THE TWISTED CLAW

A series of museum thefts launch the Hardy Boys on this baffling mystery. Rare collections of ancient pirate treasure are being stolen. Who is doing it? And how is the loot being smuggled out of the United States?

Frank and Joe's celebrated detective father is working on the case and asks the boys to stake out the *Black Parrot,* a suspicious freighter docked in Bayport Harbor. Disguised as crewmen the teen-age sleuths board the ship, determined to investigate its cargo hold.

Clues that the boys unearth take them on a whirlwind chase after a self-styled pirate king—a chase that leads to their imprisonment in the fantastic Caribbean island stronghold of the Empire of the Twisted Claw. How Frank and Joe cleverly outmaneuver the pirate king and his cohorts makes a gripping tale of suspense and high adventure.

Frank grabbed the steel girder just in time!

Hardy Boys Mystery Stories

THE
TWISTED
CLAW

BY

FRANKLIN W. DIXON

NEW YORK
GROSSET & DUNLAP
Publishers

CONTENTS

THE
TWISTED
CLAW

CHAPTER I

Shadowed!

"Congratulations!" Frank Hardy shouted to his brother Joe as the track meet ended. "You've won the trophy for Bayport High and set a new record for the hundred-yard dash!"

"You helped, too," Joe called, jogging along the cinder track. "What about your gold medal in the 440?" he said as he came to a halt.

"Don't forget me!" exclaimed Chet Morton. He was a stout, round-faced youth and a good friend of the Hardys. "I collected a few points in the shot-put."

"You were great, Chet," Frank said with a grin.

The trio had taken part in the annual track-and-field meet with Hopkinsville at a stadium near their home town of Bayport. The contest also marked the beginning of summer vacation.

"Well, are we going over to the soda shop to celebrate?" Chet asked.

"Sure, some of the other guys want to come, too," Joe replied. "Let's go and change—"

He was interrupted by an announcement over the loudspeaker. "Frank and Joe Hardy to the telephone, please."

"Oh, oh. We'd better forget about the celebration," Frank said. "Let's go, Joe."

They went to the manager's office, who handed Frank the phone. "It's your father," he said.

Frank scooped it up. "Hello, Dad. We won!"

"Nice going." There was a pause. "Frank," Mr. Hardy went on, "I'd like you and Joe to come home soon. It's important."

Within minutes the boys had showered and changed and were in their convertible, driving toward Bayport.

"I hope there's nothing wrong," Joe remarked anxiously.

"I don't think so," Frank answered. "I have a hunch it has something to do with a new case."

Their father, Fenton Hardy, had once been a member of the New York City police force. But now he was engaged in private practice as a detective and was often assisted by his sons. Working as a team, they had solved many baffling crimes, beginning with *The Tower Treasure*. Their last case was *The Secret Warning*, which had added even more renown to the Hardy name.

"Hi, Mother," the boys called when they arrived home.

Mrs. Hardy, an attractive, soft-spoken woman, greeted her sons with a smile. "How did the meet go?" she inquired.

"Just great!" Joe declared. "We won the trophy!"

"We'll tell you about it later," Frank interrupted. "Where's Dad?"

"Upstairs. He's waiting for you."

The boys rushed to the second floor and entered their father's study. He was seated at his desk. Mr. Hardy was a distinguished-looking man who appeared much younger than his years.

"We came as fast as we could," Frank said.

"Thanks," Mr. Hardy replied. "I wouldn't have called if it wasn't important. I'm going to need your help in connection with a new case."

"What did I tell you!" Frank exclaimed as he playfully slapped his brother on the shoulder.

"What kind of a case?" Joe asked eagerly.

"I can't go into detail at this point. Besides, I'll be leaving on a trip shortly," his father said. "Here it is briefly. Right now there is a ship in Bayport Harbor called the *Black Parrot*. I know nothing about it other than it might have some connection with my case. I'd like you to keep an eye on the freighter while it's in port. Record anything about the crew or cargo that looks even slightly suspicious."

Frank, dark-haired and eighteen, a year older

than his blond brother, looked at his father quizzically. "That sounds sort of tame, Dad."

"I know. But it could turn out to be a pretty
wild case, as you boys say."

"Should we contact you if we find any information?"

"No. I'll get in touch with you."

At that instant Mrs. Hardy entered the room.
"Fenton," she said nervously, "I'm worried.
There's a man across the street. I'm sure he's
watching our house. He's hiding behind a tree,
but I caught several glimpses of him."

Joe, the more impetuous of the brothers,
jumped to his feet. "Let's go and have a talk with
that guy. We'll soon find out what he's up to!"

"Hold it!" Mr. Hardy ordered. "It's possible he
has been assigned to shadow me. I don't want him
to know he has been spotted. It'll put his cohorts
on guard."

Joe nodded. "This *must* be quite a case. Wish
you could tell us more about it."

The detective did not answer. He glanced at his
watch. "I'm due at the airport soon. Somehow I've
got to get out of the house without being seen."

"How about the back door?" Joe suggested.

"No good," his father said. "Chances are there's
another man posted behind the house."

"Maybe some kind of a disguise would work,"
Frank said.

"I'm afraid it would be a bit too obvious under

the circumstances," Mr. Hardy replied. "Unless someone—" His words trailed off as he reached for the telephone book, looked up a number, and dialed. "I'm going to call Mr. Callahan and ask him to come over right away."

"Our plumber?" Joe asked.

The boys glanced at each other in bewilderment. What could their father possibly want with a plumber at this time?

"You'll see," Mr. Hardy said with a wink.

About ten minutes later a small panel truck came to a stop in front of the Hardy home. Mr. Callahan, a middle-aged man wearing a visor cap and overalls, climbed out. He had a rather large nose and bushy eyebrows.

He walked toward the house, carrying a tool kit in his right hand. The young detectives led him to their father's study, where Mr. Hardy quickly told him of his predicament.

"Now this is my plan, Mr. Callahan," Mr. Hardy continued. "You and I are about the same size and weight. If you'll lend me your cap and overalls for a while, I can disguise myself well enough to pass as your double—at least at a distance."

The plumber was an old acquaintance and readily agreed. They left the study and went to the master bedroom. A few minutes later they reappeared. With a putty nose and false eyebrows Mr. Hardy looked amazingly like Callahan.

"A good makeup job, Dad!" Frank exclaimed. "You and Mr. Callahan could be twin brothers."

At that instant Gertrude Hardy entered the room. She was the tall, angular, peppery sister of Mr. Hardy. "My word! I'm seeing double!" she exclaimed. "Two Mr. Callahans in this room!"

"You're not seeing double," Joe assured her with a laugh. "One of them is Dad in disguise."

"And a pretty good likeness too, don't you think?" Frank added.

Aunt Gertrude turned to face the plumber. "Fenton, what on earth are you up to now? Something to do with a new case I take it. One day something awful is going to happen. I'm sure of it!"

Mr. Hardy stepped forward. "I'm afraid you're scolding the wrong man."

Aunt Gertrude shook her head and marched out of the room. The boys roared with laughter.

"Now back to the business at hand," Mr. Hardy said. "I'll leave here in Mr. Callahan's truck. You boys take him to the airport in an hour to pick it up. Please bill me for the time, Mr. Callahan."

"I won't think of it. It's a favor," the plumber said.

"I insist," said Mr. Hardy, then addressed his sons, "Any questions before I leave?"

"No, Dad," Joe replied.

"Let's hope," the detective continued, "that our friend across the street falls for my trick."

"The trick worked!" Frank exclaimed triumphantly

After saying good-by to his family, he picked up the plumber's tool kit, took a deep breath, and left the house.

The boys cautiously peered through a window. Across the street they saw a man's head pop out from behind a tree, then vanish again as their father drove off. Obviously the stranger was remaining at his post.

"The trick worked!" Frank exclaimed triumphantly.

"Right," Joe agreed. "But I wonder how long that guy is going to stick around."

Frank chuckled. "One thing is certain. He's in for a long wait."

While Aunt Gertrude prepared a cup of tea for Mr. Callahan, Frank and Joe discussed the case.

"The *Black Parrot*," Joe mused. "Sounds eerie."

"Let's go down to the harbor first thing in the morning," Frank said. "Right now we'd better keep an eye on that fellow across the street."

The boys hurried downstairs and peered through one of the living-room windows. Minutes passed.

"No sign of him," Joe muttered. "Maybe he's gone."

"Could be," his brother replied. "But let's wait a while longer, just to be sure."

While Frank kept his post at the window, Joe paced up and down impatiently. Finally he could not suppress his curiosity any longer. "I'm going to see if that spy's still there," he said and ran out of the house. He looked behind the tree across the street, then signaled Frank that the coast was clear.

When he came back Frank met him at the door. "You shouldn't have run out like that, you know."

"Sorry. I thought it was about time for a show-down."

"You might have—"

Frank was interrupted by a terrifying scream from the kitchen.

CHAPTER II

The Black Parrot

"HOLY crow!" Joe exclaimed. "That was Aunt Gertrude!"

The boys rushed into the kitchen and almost collided with their mother who had heard the scream, too.

They found Miss Hardy shaking like a leaf. She pointed to an open window. "A-a strange man was looking in at me! Call the police! Do something!"

Frank and Joe spotted a man running down the street. They dashed out of the house and gave chase, but before they could close the gap, their quarry leaped into a car and sped off.

"There were two men in that car!" Frank declared. "One of them must have been watching the rear of the house as Dad suspected. He tried to get a look inside and frightened the wits out of Aunty."

"I wonder what he was up to," Joe put in.

"Your guess is as good as mine," Frank replied.

They returned to find their mother pressing a cold wet towel on Aunt Gertrude's forehead.

"How do you feel?" Joe inquired.

"Awful! Simply awful!" exclaimed Aunt Gertrude. "Who was that cutthroat?"

"Probably just a peddler," Frank replied, hoping not to upset her further. "Your scream frightened him more than he frightened you."

"Some nerve!" Aunt Gertrude snapped. "Imagine! Peering into people's houses."

Frank looked at his watch. "I think we can leave now," he said to Mr. Callahan. "Come on. We'll take you to the airport to pick up your truck."

"Okay." As they got into the boys' convertible, the plumber said, "Tell me, is there always that much excitement at your house?"

Frank winked at his brother. "This is a rather quiet day, wouldn't you say, Joe?"

Mr. Callahan shook his head and asked no more questions.

The boys retired early that night and were up at six the next morning. After breakfast they drove to Bayport Harbor. They found the area bustling with activity.

"There's the *Black Parrot*," Joe said, pointing.

They watched as stevedores pushed handcarts, loaded with wooden crates, up a gangplank to the ship. A hoist was putting heavier cargo aboard.

"We won't be able to get much information for Dad unless we can board the ship," Joe remarked.

Frank did not speak. Instead, he signaled Joe to follow him and walked toward a crewman who was standing at the base of the gangplank checking a manifest.

"My brother and I are very much interested in ships," Frank began nonchalantly. "Do you think your captain would let us go aboard for a few minutes?"

The man glared at them in surprise. "Get outta here!" he roared.

"Why get mad at us?" Joe queried. "We were just—"

"You heard me! Get outta here before I take a club to ya!"

Joe was about to challenge the man, but Frank grabbed his brother's arm and led him away from the ship.

"That guy's about as pleasant as a rattlesnake," Joe said angrily.

"Take it easy," Frank warned. "We can't risk getting involved in a row. We've got to remain as inconspicuous as possible."

"What'll we do now?"

"Wait and hope for a break."

The young detectives watched the *Black Parrot* from a distance. Then came a stroke of luck. A crewman placed a sign at the base of the gangplank announcing that more help was needed to load the ship. The Hardys were among the first to volunteer.

"So! It's you two again!" growled the man they had encountered earlier. He stared at them for a moment. "Well—you kids look pretty strong." He named a price for every crate carried aboard and told them to take it or leave it.

"We'll take it," Frank said quickly. "But what about union cards?"

"Forget the union and get movin'!" the crewman ordered. "We haven't got any more handcarts, so you'll have to bring the crates aboard one by one."

"Thanks a lot," Joe muttered.

The job was extremely hard. The boys stuck to it most of the day, hoping to learn something, but their sleuthing was hampered by the constant surveillance of the crew.

That afternoon, while carrying a crate aboard, Joe tripped and fell. The wooden box crashed to the deck. At that instant the first mate of the *Black Parrot* appeared and demanded to know what was going on.

"Just an accident," Frank explained. "My brother tripped and—"

"I'm not interested in excuses!" the officer yelled. He gave Joe a shove. "Now pick that up. And be quick about it!"

"Pick it up yourself!" Joe retorted as he scrambled to his feet.

The first mate was about to lash out with his fist, but Frank stepped in and grabbed him by the arm. As he did, he noticed that the man was wearing a strange ring on his finger. It consisted of a heavy silver band with what looked like a red, twisted bird's claw on top.

"Let go of my arm!" the man demanded. Frank released him. "Now get your pay and get off the ship!"

"We haven't finished our work," Joe said.

Several crewmen moved toward the Hardys. "You heard him," one of them snarled. "Get goin'."

The boys had no choice but to comply.

Joe sighed. "I certainly messed things up."

"It wasn't your fault," Frank said. "Anyway, we couldn't have done much investigating with all those guys around."

As they walked down the gangplank to the pier, they heard a familiar voice call out, "Hi, masterminds!" It was Chet Morton. "Your mother said you were down here," he went on. "What're you doing?"

Frank and Joe drew the stout boy aside and told him about their assignment and their adventure onboard.

"And you fellows were ordered off the ship, eh?" Chet reflected. "Let me see." He began walking toward the *Black Parrot*. "I'll get some information for you."

"Wait a minute!" Frank said. "Come back here!" His words went unheeded.

"Ahoy, mates! Make way for a real seaman!" Chet shouted to a group of crewmen as he hurried up the gangplank.

"Oh, oh. Now we're really in for trouble," Joe muttered anxiously.

Chet disappeared into the midst of the group. Shortly scuffling broke out among the men. Before Frank and Joe could aid their friend, he came rolling down the gangplank like an oversized bowling ball.

"Are you all right?" Frank cried as he and Joe rushed to Chet.

The stout youth got to his feet and began brushing off his clothes. "I'm—I'm okay. Those guys aren't very friendly."

Frank frowned. "Right now, our chances of getting back aboard the ship are nil. Let's go home and try to figure out another plan."

The boys had an early supper, then went to their father's study to discuss their next move.

Joe thought for a moment. "I've got an idea," he said finally. "Why don't we disguise ourselves as a couple of crewmen and just board the ship?"

"I don't know," Frank muttered, rubbing his chin dubiously. "Then again, it might work if we try it after dark."

"I'll dig up the caps and seamen's jackets we used on that sailing trip last year."

"Okay. But let's disguise ourselves in the car. We don't want Mother and Aunt Gertrude to see us. They'll only worry."

The boys lost no time putting their plan into action. Within half an hour they had completed their disguise.

"You look as if you've been at sea for years," Frank said laughingly as he gazed at his brother.

Joe grinned as he started the car. "And no one would take you for a landlubber either."

It had been dark for nearly an hour when the Hardys arrived at the harbor. They were startled to find the *Black Parrot* gone.

Frank leaped out of the convertible and approached a watchman who was walking along the pier. "Where's the *Black Parrot?*" he asked.

The man eyed the young detective. "Sailed about an hour ago. Were you supposed to be on board?"

"Er—no," Frank replied. "Heard the ship was in port. Just wondered if the captain needed a couple of extra hands."

"Then you ain't missed nothin'," the watchman told him. "Strangest crew I ever did see. Weren't friendly toward nobody. You'd be better off signin' on with another ship. Try the *Nomad*. It'll be dockin' here in the mornin'."

Frank hurried back to the car. "Well, that's that." He sighed. "The ship's gone and we have nothing to report to Dad."

"This was a tough assignment," Joe commented. "If only we had had more time."

They removed their disguises and returned home. Aunt Gertrude had a message for them. "Your father telephoned while you were gone. He wants you to get a book for him."

"Sure," Frank said. "What is it?"

"It's called *Essays in Criminology,* by Weaver. He said you might have some trouble finding it since it's out of print."

"We'll try. How's Dad?"

"Fine. He'll call again in a few days."

The boys spent the following day canvassing the second-hand bookstores in Bayport. Their search was unsuccessful, however.

"Let's go to New York City," Frank suggested. "If there's a copy of the *Essays* anywhere, we're likely to find it there."

That evening Joe telephoned Jack Wayne, pilot of Mr. Hardy's single-engine aircraft. The plane was based at Bayport Airport. Wayne readily agreed to fly the boys to New York.

"By the way, I understand your father recently left on a trip by airline," the pilot said jokingly. "What's wrong? Doesn't he like his own plane any more?"

"Not necessarily," Joe answered with a laugh. "Maybe he thought you needed a vacation. We'll see you in the morning."

The following day was crisp and clear. Jack

Wayne was already warming up the plane's engine when the Hardys arrived at the airport. Soon they were off the ground and headed for their destination. A little more than two hours later the pilot made a smooth landing at La Guardia Airport.

Frank and Joe got on a bus that took them into the city. There they looked in the classified telephone directory and made more than a dozen calls to various bookstores, but to no avail.

Finally they went to a street well known for second-hand bookstores. After hours of searching, they finally discovered a copy of the book their father wanted.

"What luck!" Frank exclaimed as he flipped through its pages.

Joe, meanwhile, glanced casually toward the rare-book section. Suddenly his eyes fastened on a certain volume. He grabbed Frank's shoulder. "Look! Over there!"

CHAPTER III

Trapped at Sea

"It's the symbol!" Frank exclaimed. "Just like the one I saw on the first mate's ring!"

The boys stared at an old volume entitled *Empire of the Twisted Claw*. The strange, red-colored insignia was stamped on its cover. Thick glass doors with sturdy locks prevented the Hardys from examining the book more closely.

At that moment the proprietor of the shop appeared. "Find something that interests you?" he inquired.

"How much are you asking for that book?" Joe asked.

The man adjusted his eyeglasses and peered at the volume. "I'll have to look up the exact price. But nothing on this shelf goes for less than fifteen hundred dollars."

Frank and Joe looked glum. Buying the book was out of the question.

The proprietor saw that they were greatly disappointed. He regarded them for a moment, then smiled. "Tell you what. Promise to be careful, and I'll let you see the volume."

The Hardys were elated. They thanked the man as he pulled the book from the shelf and placed it on a reading table nearby.

"It's dated 1786," Frank observed as he and Joe examined the opening page.

The text that followed revealed a fascinating story. It concerned the adventures of an early eighteenth-century pirate named Cartoll. The sight of his ship, the *Black Parrot,* struck fear into those who sailed the Atlantic trade routes of that era.

"Good grief!" Joe exclaimed. "Whoever named the freighter we tried to investigate must've known about Cartoll."

"Kind of weird. What do you make of it?" Frank asked.

"I don't know. Let's go back to the story."

Reading on, the boys learned that Cartoll discovered an island somewhere in the Caribbean. He used it not only as a base of operations for his pirating activities, but also for the creation of a private kingdom. Cartoll referred to his realm as the Empire of the Twisted Claw.

"Wow!" Joe declared. "He certainly was an ambitious guy."

"It says here," Frank stated as he ran his finger along the page, "that the few natives on the island were forced to become his subjects. Later, his kingdom was enlarged by bringing captives there from the ships he had plundered."

The story also revealed that Cartoll had formed an elite personal guard. Each of the men had the symbol of the twisted claw on the breastplate of his armor.

As the Hardys turned the next page, they found that the remainder of the text was so faded it was impossible to read. Apparently the last section of the volume had been damaged by seawater.

"Bad luck." Frank sighed. "I was hoping we'd learn more about Cartoll and where his island was located."

"If we could take the book to our crime lab," Joe suggested, "the rest of the text might show up under ultraviolet light."

"The owner will never go along with it," Frank replied.

"What've we got to lose? Let's try, anyway."

The proprietor flatly refused their request. He quickly placed the book back on its shelf. "You fellows must think I'm crazy!"

"Not at all, sir," Frank said apologetically. "We can't tell you why at the moment, but it's important that we see the rest of the text."

"Only the buyer of that book will leave my

shop with it!" the man snapped. "Anyway, I'd never permit it to be exposed to chemicals and lights."

The young detectives decided not to press the issue any further. They paid for the volume of essays and started back to the airport.

"I wonder if there's another copy of that *Twisted Claw* book around somewhere," Joe remarked as Wayne lifted the plane off the runway at La Guardia.

Frank glanced at his brother. "The bookshop owner claimed that it's the only one known to be in existence. If there *is* another one, it could take years to track it down."

It was early evening when they arrived home. After supper Frank settled down to look at the book they had bought for their father. Joe, meanwhile, leafed through the evening newspaper.

Suddenly he sat bolt upright in his chair. "Frank! We're due for a break! This is great!"

"What are you talking about?"

"There's an item here which says the *Black Parrot* has developed engine trouble and is returning to Bayport Harbor for repairs!"

"When?"

"Sometime tomorrow afternoon," Joe replied, tossing the paper to his brother.

Frank read the article. "According to this, the captain doesn't expect repairs to take more than twenty-four hours."

"This might be our last chance to investigate the ship," Joe said. "We'll have to work fast."

The following afternoon the boys drove to Bayport Harbor, hopeful that the ship would arrive as scheduled. Their spirits soared when they spotted the *Black Parrot* easing into a dock.

Members of the crew spilled down the gangplank to help secure the lines.

"Let's stick to our original plan," Frank suggested. "We'll disguise ourselves as seamen again and board the ship after dark."

"Meanwhile, I'll call Chet and ask him to meet us here later," Joe said.

As night approached, the young detectives began putting on their disguise and facial makeup. They finished just as Chet arrived. Their friend was dumbfounded when he saw his two chums.

"How do we look?" Joe asked him.

"Great!" Chet declared. "You'd fool anybody into thinking you're a couple of old salts."

The Hardys then told him what they wanted him to do. "And remember," Frank urged, "stay out of sight and keep your eyes open. Don't run for help unless we really get into a tough spot."

"Roger. You can count on me," Chet replied.

The boys braced themselves and started down the pier toward the *Black Parrot*. They climbed the gangplank and stepped onto the deck.

A crewman came toward them. He stopped and

glanced at the youths. "I ain't seen you guys aboard before."

Frank mumbled in doubletalk.

"Better check with the first mate then," the fellow advised. "You'll find him in the forward galley."

"Thanks," Joe replied.

The crewman continued on his way. Casually the boys walked along the deck for a short distance, then dashed down a passageway.

"Whew!" Joe sighed. "That was close. I was afraid that guy would insist on taking us to the first mate."

Frank creased his brow. "There's a chance he might check later to see if we did report. We'd better not risk staying aboard too long."

"What should we investigate first?"

"The cargo hold. I'd like to see what sort of load they're carrying."

Stealthily they made their way midships, pulled open a hatch, and descended a ladder into the cargo hold. Taking out their flashlights, the boys began to scan the area. The room was filled with wooden crates. They carefully pried the top off one of the boxes and found that it contained a coil of electric cable.

Examination of the labels on other crates indicated that the merchandise varied from leather goods to automobile parts. Most of the shipments were slated for Iceland.

"So far," Frank remarked, "there's nothing suspicious about this cargo."

"Maybe it's all a cover-up for some kind of an illegal operation," Joe said.

As they continued their search, the beam of Joe's flashlight fell upon a metal enclosure. It formed a small, separate room at the far end of the hold.

"Wonder what's in there," Joe said.

"Let's take a look," Frank suggested.

The Hardys unlatched the door of the enclosure and went inside.

Joe let out a low whistle. "More crates. And they're marked 'Explosives'!"

Frank tugged at the top of a box. "We'd need a long crowbar to break into one of these."

Suddenly the area outside the enclosure was filled with light and crewmen descended the ladder into the hold.

The boys listened anxiously as one of the men shouted an order to the others. "Double check to see everything is secure!"

Frank and Joe held their breath. The door of the enclosure was partially open. They stiffened at the sound of approaching footsteps.

"Hey!" a man yelled. "Someone left the door to the special storeroom unlatched. Won't you guys ever learn?"

An instant later the door was slammed shut. The Hardys were left in total darkness.

BOOKMOBILE

Frank switched on his flashlight. "Oh, oh. Now we're in for it. There's no latch on the inside. We're trapped!"

"Wh-what'll we do?" Joe stammered.

"Either yell for help and get caught, or wait until the hold is clear and try to find a way out. What say?"

"Let's wait."

Ten minutes later they heard the men leave.

"Okay, let's move some of this stuff to see if there's another exit," Frank suggested.

He placed his flashlight on the floor near the door and with Joe's help moved the heavy crates away from the walls. The work was backbreaking, but to no avail. There were no other doors!

Dripping with perspiration, the Hardys sat down on the floor and leaned against a crate to ponder their next move. As Joe made himself comfortable, his fingers touched an object and he picked it up.

"Hey," he cried out, "look what I found!"

Frank beamed his light on a large screwdriver which Joe held in his hand.

"Maybe we can open the latch with this," Frank said. "Here, let me have it." He scrambled up and tried to ram the tool through the narrow slit between the door and the wall. No luck. The screwdriver was much too thick.

"Oh, nuts!" Joe said.

"Let's see if we can't locate something else," Frank said hopefully.

They shifted the crates again and scoured the floor. Their hands were black with dirt, and they coughed as dust assailed their nostrils. But not another tool was to be found.

"I guess we'll just have to wait until someone comes down again, and then play it by ear," Joe muttered.

Presently the boys sensed a strong vibration. The engines of the *Black Parrot* had been started.

"The ship's getting underway!" Joe exclaimed.

CHAPTER IV

Good Old Chet

"WE'VE got to get out of here!" Frank declared.

The Hardys tried to force the door, but their efforts were useless. They thought of Chet. Would he give the alarm? Perhaps he'd send the Coast Guard to free them.

Finally, drowsy because of the lack of fresh air, they dozed off. Hours passed before they awoke.

Frank glanced at his watch. "The ship must be eighty or ninety miles out of Bayport by now," he said weakly.

"We can't stay in here much longer," Joe answered. He was breathing heavily. "Our only chance is to let them know we're in the storeroom."

"You're right. Start pounding on the door. We're bound to attract someone's attention."

Each of the boys removed one of their shoes and

used it to hammer away at the door. But no one heard them.

"It's no use," Joe muttered in despair.

They were ready to give up, when Frank suddenly whispered tensely, "Wait! I hear footsteps!"

An instant later the door was pulled open. The boys found themselves facing three startled crewmen.

"Who are you?" one of them demanded. "Watcha doin' in here?"

The Hardys did not answer. Hungrily they gulped in fresh air.

"Stowaways, eh?" the man snarled. "The cap'n will know how to deal with you!" He stared at the youths curiously. "What's that you got on your faces?"

Frank and Joe glanced at each other. They realized with dismay that the hours they had spent in the warm, stagnant air of the enclosure had caused their makeup to streak. They had no choice but to remove it completely.

"Why, they're a couple of kids!" one of the men shouted in surprise.

The boys were ordered to march off with one of the crew members leading the way to the captain. He was a middle-aged man with a thin beard and skin that looked as tough as an elephant's hide. His eyes were deep-set and piercing. The Hardys felt uncomfortable in his presence.

"Cap'n," the crewman reported, "we found these two guys hidin' in the special storeroom."

"What were you doing there?" the officer demanded. "How did you get aboard?"

At that moment the first mate appeared on the scene. His eyes widened with surprise when he saw the Hardys. "What are those troublemakers doin' here?" he thundered.

"You know them?" the captain asked.

"Yes, sir. Had to run them off the ship when we were takin' on cargo in Bayport Harbor. They asked for work and I hired them to help load. Then that blond-haired one tried to pick a fight with me."

"You've no right shoving people around!" Joe said.

"Quiet!" the captain shouted. "Now that you're aboard, you'll stay. And you'll work without pay."

"We demand you let us off this ship!" Frank exclaimed.

The first mate roared with laughter. "It's a long swim back to Bayport!"

"What's your next port?" Joe asked. "We'll go ashore there."

"None of your business," the captain retorted. "What's more, if you give us any trouble you won't eat. Now I'm turning you over to my first mate. His name is Marik. You'll be responsible to him."

"I warn you," Frank protested. "You'll regret it if you try to keep us aboard!"

Marik stepped forward and shoved them on ahead of him. "Stow the talk and get goin'. We can use a couple of hands in the galley. Some hard work will take the starch out of you."

When they arrived in the galley, the first mate ordered the Hardys to begin scrubbing the floor. "I want the job finished before the cooks come on duty to start breakfast. That gives you only an hour."

"But we need some sleep and food!" Joe protested.

"No back talk!" Marik growled.

Frank and Joe were given brushes and pails. They finished their task just minutes before the cooks appeared.

"So you're the stowaways Marik told me about," one of the men boomed. "I've got orders to see that you're kept busy. Look lively now!"

As soon as one galley chore was completed, the boys were assigned another. The aroma of food nearly drove them mad with hunger. Finally they were permitted a few moments to eat.

When they had finished, one of the cooks shouted to Frank, "Hey, you! Take this tray of food to the skipper!"

Frank picked it up. As he approached the captain's cabin he heard voices inside. Cautiously he pressed his ear against the door.

"I don't like havin' those kids aboard, Cap'n," a man grumbled. Frank recognized the voice. It was Marik. "They might be a couple of snoopers tryin' to find out about the setup."

"Stop worrying," was the reply. "They're just stowaways looking for a free ride. Well, that's what they're going to get. They won't get off this ship till we reach the island."

"You're takin' 'em all the way?" Marik asked. "I hope you know what you're doin'."

"Leave it to me. But just to be safe, lock the kids up in the storeroom when we put into Stormwell tomorrow morning."

"Stormwell!" Frank thought. "That's a port on the Canadian coast!" He waited a few seconds before knocking on the cabin door. Summoned by the captain to enter, he delivered the tray, then hurried back to the galley.

It was late evening before the boys had an opportunity to talk. Frank told his brother what he had overheard.

"So! They intend to keep us prisoners!" Joe said angrily.

"Yes! Somehow we've got to make it ashore when the ship docks at Stormwell!"

"Slim chance of that if we're locked in the storeroom."

Frank thought a moment. "We've one thing in our favor," he said finally. "The captain and Marik don't know we're onto them. And they're not planning to lock us up until the ship docks, or shortly before—"

"I get it!" Joe interrupted. "We'll wait till the last minute, then make a break for it."

Just then the boys heard footsteps. They whirled around to see Marik and four crewmen walking toward them.

"I've been watchin' you guys," the first mate growled. "You're up to somethin'."

"What do you mean?" Frank asked.

"Shut up!" Marik shouted fiercely. "The cap'n gave me orders to lock you up in the mornin'. But I'm not takin' any chances. You're goin' to the storeroom right now!"

"That's what you think!" Joe protested. He flung himself at the first mate and together they went crashing to the deck.

Frank joined in the fight. He bent low and rammed his shoulder into the midriff of one of the crewmen. Then he struck out with a blow that sent another hurtling against the bulkhead. The melee attracted more members of the crew. Outnumbered, the Hardys were finally subdued.

"Take 'em to the storeroom!" Marik yelled as he struggled to his feet.

The boys were marched off to the cargo hold and shoved into the metal-walled enclosure. Then the door was slammed shut and locked.

"It'll take a miracle to get us out of this," Joe said.

Though hours dragged by, Frank and Joe were only able to sleep for short periods. They were anxious about what would happen next. Glumly they talked of Chet. Maybe something had befallen him, too. Perhaps he never had a chance to report where they were!

Frank glanced at the luminous dial on his watch. "Holy crow! It's morning. Nearly eight o'clock!"

"Listen!" Joe said. "The ship's engines. They're slowing down."

"We must be putting into Stormwell."

"If only we could get out of here!"

For a while there were sounds of activity on the deck above. Then, almost an hour passed before they heard footsteps again.

The storeroom door was pulled open. A crewman ordered the youths to follow him and led them up on deck. Two Canadian policemen were standing with the captain of the *Black Parrot*.

"Are you the lads from Bayport?" one of them asked.

"Yes!" the Hardys answered excitedly.

"Stowaways, you mean!" the captain barked. "I locked them up to teach them a lesson. We were going to put them ashore later."

"Liar," Joe muttered.

The policemen ushered the boys down the gangplank and toward a waiting car.

"Hello, sons," came a familiar voice from inside the vehicle. "Climb in."

"Dad!" Frank cried out, nearly speechless.

"What—what are you doing here?" stammered Joe. "How did you know where we—?"

Mr. Hardy grinned. "Get into the car and I'll explain."

As they drove off, the detective told his sons that he had been working in Montreal in connection with his case. By coincidence he had telephoned home only seconds after Chet had arrived to inform Mrs. Hardy that Frank and Joe had sailed off in the *Black Parrot*.

"Good old Chet!" Joe exclaimed.

"He didn't take immediate action," Mr. Hardy said, "because he thought it might be part of your plan to sail with the ship a short distance, then dive overboard. But he began to worry after an hour and decided to tell your mother what had happened."

"Lucky for us," Frank commented.

Their father went on to say that he checked with Bayport Harbor and learned that the *Black Parrot* was to make a stop in Stormwell.

"And so," Mr. Hardy concluded, "I requested the help of the Canadian police, just in case the captain had any ideas about making you boys permanent members of the crew."

"And he decided to turn us loose," Joe added, "rather than risk an investigation."

"That's just what I hoped would happen," Mr. Hardy said.

He noticed Frank's eyelids start to droop. "Try to catch a few winks," he went on. "We'll continue our discussion when we get to Montreal."

When they arrived, the detective obtained accommodations for Frank and Joe at the hotel where he was staying. The boys slept for a few hours, then had dinner served in their room. Their father entered as they finished eating.

"Feeling better?"

"I'll say," Joe assured him.

"And now, Dad, we'd like to tell you what information we dug up," Frank began, and they described their adventures aboard the *Black Parrot*. Then they informed their father that they had found the book he wanted and about the rare volume they had looked at in the New York bookstore.

Mr. Hardy was stunned. "An island kingdom called the Empire of the Twisted Claw, you say?"

"Yes," Frank answered. "It was ruled by a pirate named Cartoll."

The detective began to pace the floor. Finally he spoke. "What an amazing story. And it seems to tie in with my case!"

"How?" Frank asked.

"I'm not certain yet. But from what you told me, this might prove to be one of the strangest mysteries we've ever encountered!"

CHAPTER V

Solo Assignments

FRANK and Joe waited in anticipation as their father settled into a chair opposite them.

"Boys," Mr. Hardy began, "I've been engaged by the Reed Museum Association to investigate a series of thefts. Four museums have been robbed within a few days, three in the United States and the Abbey Museum here in Montreal."

"What were the thieves after? Gems? Precious metals?" questioned Frank.

"That's one of the strange facts about the case," the detective explained. "Each of the museums had a portion of the DeGraw collection on display. It was only those items that were stolen. Nothing else in the buildings was touched."

"What's the DeGraw collection?" Joe queried.

Mr. Hardy explained that Elden DeGraw was a wealthy financier who took an interest in archaeology. Several years before, he had discovered a sunken galleon in the Caribbean. The ship was filled with priceless royal treasure, including scepters, crowns, and orbs. Of particular interest were suits of armor which had red, twisted claw symbols on their breastplates."

"Wow!" Joe exclaimed. "The armor might have belonged to Cartoll's elite guard!"

Mr. Hardy leaned forward. "That's why I was a bit stunned when you told me the story about the pirate and his Empire of the Twisted Claw."

"Are there any other museums that have portions of the collection?" Frank asked.

"Yes," his father replied. "DeGraw divided up the items and donated them to ten different museums—the Abbey Museum here and nine in the United States."

"Do you think the thieves will try to rob the other six?" Joe inquired.

"I'm sure of it," Mr. Hardy said.

He then told his sons that he had a hunch the loot was being taken out of the country, but how was a mystery. Each portion of the collection was bulky and would be difficult to smuggle.

"I considered the possibility of a ship being involved," Mr. Hardy continued. "Checking, I learned that the freighter *Black Parrot* and its sister ship *Yellow Parrot* were suspected of carrying on some sort of illegal operation. But no one has ever come up with a shred of evidence. That's why I asked you to investigate."

"Without much success," Frank muttered dejectedly.

"At least we know Dad's hunch was right," Joe put in.

"Hold it," Mr. Hardy ordered with a grin. "There's lots to learn about the case before making any conclusions."

The boys accompanied their father to the scene of the recent theft. The curator of the Abbey Museum was greatly upset over the loss of the collection. "I don't understand how they could have gotten into the building without setting off the alarm," he said.

"I don't either," Mr. Hardy admitted. "The system wasn't tampered with and is in perfect working order."

At that moment the telephone rang. The curator picked up the instrument, then handed it to Mr. Hardy. "It's for you. Mr. Hertford of the Reed Museum Association."

The detective stiffened when he heard what his caller had to say. Finally he hung up and turned to the boys. "We're flying to New York immediately! The Standon Museum has been robbed. Its portion of the DeGraw collection is gone!"

The Hardys quickly made airline reservations and were on their way within the hour. When they arrived at the museum, the young detectives assisted their father in searching for clues.

"Hm! This robbery is like all the others," Mr.

Hardy observed. "The alarm system is intact, and there's been a clean sweep of the collection."

"How does the system work?" Frank asked.

"When turned on," his father explained, "invisible beams of light crisscross the exhibit rooms from all directions just inches above the floor. It operates on the photoelectric cell principle."

"I get it!" Joe interrupted. "Anyone walking into the room would break the light beams and set off the alarm."

"Pretty effective," Frank added. "A thief would have to be able to float through the air like a balloon to escape detection."

Mr. Hardy nodded. "I'd give anything to know the gang's *modus operandi*."

After completing their investigation, the Hardys spent the night in New York, then returned to Bayport the following morning. The boys joined their father in his study to hear a plan he had in mind.

"Five museums still have their DeGraw collections," Mr. Hardy said. "And we don't know which is next on the thieves' list. The local police can't spare men to be on constant surveillance, and the museum guards need help. My plan is to have each of us cover one and prevent a robbery, if possible."

"We can have Chet help us out, too," Joe suggested.

Mr. Hardy appeared somewhat dubious. "Do

you think he can handle an assignment like this?"

"I'm sure he can," Frank replied.

"All right." The detective unfolded a sheet of paper. "Here's a list of the museums. Four of them are in neighboring states. The fifth is in California. I'll have Sam Radley take care of that one."

Frank and Joe had often worked with Radley, their father's assistant, and knew he would do a good job.

Then Frank telephoned Chet to tell him about the plan. The stout boy was jubilant.

"I'm ready to leave any time!" he declared. "It'll be a sorry day for those crooks if they try to rob the place with me on guard!"

By evening Mr. Hardy had completed all the necessary arrangements. Early the next morning Frank, Joe, Sam Radley, and Chet met in his study for a final briefing. After reviewing his plan, Mr. Hardy gave a word of warning. "Remember, we don't know where the thieves will strike next. They're clever and dangerous. So don't take any chances."

After wishing each other luck, they started out on their individual assignments. Frank was to cover a museum in Philadelphia. He arrived in the afternoon and introduced himself to the curator, Bruce Watkins.

"Ah, yes," said the scholarly-looking official. "Your father phoned that you were coming. I feel comforted that such famous detectives as the Hardys are investigating the recent robberies."

"Thank you," Frank said. "Now, if you don't mind, I'd like to see your DeGraw collection."

The curator led him through a series of exhibit rooms. It was a magnificent old building with marble columns and floors. They entered a large room filled with ancient artifacts. One section of it contained the DeGraw collection.

"Here we are," the curator announced.

Frank stared in awe at the scepters, crowns, and orbs displayed in a large glass case. Then his attention was drawn to a suit of armor with a red, twisted claw symbol on the breastplate.

"This is our most popular exhibit," the curator said proudly.

Frank examined his surroundings. "What kind of an alarm system do you have here?" he queried.

"The windows, doors, and most of the glass cases are well-protected," the man answered. "We are planning to install a photoelectric cell just as soon as appropriations are made available to us."

"What about guards at night?"

"We have four, but will get more from an agency as soon as we can."

At that moment a staff member told the curator that he was wanted on the phone. He excused himself and hurried off.

Frank returned to the DeGraw collection and

"This is our most popular exhibit," Watkins said

examined it more closely. Then he strolled around the other rooms. He entered one which contained large monoliths from a Pacific island, and stopped for a moment to admire the exhibit.

As he stood there, one of the stone columns behind him silently began to topple forward. Frank was directly in its path!

CHAPTER VI

A Desperate Moment

FRANK suddenly spotted the reflection of the falling column in the highly polished floor of the room. He gasped, and in a lightning move, he threw himself to one side.

Crash! The column hit the floor with an ear-splitting impact.

Frank was sprayed with bits of shattered rock as he tumbled across the floor. The curator, a guard, and several staff members came running.

"What happened?" one of them shouted.

Frank sprang to his feet. "I was almost flattened by that column," he said grimly. "It toppled over."

The curator stared in disbelief. "How could such a thing happen?"

"The column had rather a broad base," a staff member interjected. "It stood firmly in the upright position."

"Someone must have pushed it over," Frank remarked.

"Nonsense!" Watkins exclaimed, obviously startled by the suggestion. He hesitated for a moment. "Although I suppose it could be done by a man with exceptional strength."

"See here!" another staff man interrupted. "Are you suggesting that someone deliberately toppled the column?"

"Under the circumstances," Frank mused thoughtfully, "I must consider it a possibility."

"Why would anyone do such a thing?"

"For reasons I can't divulge right now," Frank replied.

He drew the curator aside. "I have a hunch this museum is next on the thieves' list. Somehow the gang must have discovered who I am, and why I'm here. Pushing that column over could have been an attempt to get me out of the way."

"Oh, come now," Watkins retorted. "Aren't you jumping to conclusions? I'm sure the whole thing was just an accident."

"All the same, we'd better assign more men to guard the DeGraw exhibit," Frank urged.

"I've already decided on another course of action," the curator said. "The entire collection will be taken to our basement storeroom immediately. It'll stay there until this whole affair of museum robberies is ended."

Watkins ordered all available staff members to

begin work at once. Nearly two hours went by before the last item of the collection was carried into the storeroom and the door securely locked by Watkins.

"I still recommend that guards be posted," Frank said. "A locked door alone is not going to stop the thieves."

"Well—all right," Watkins agreed, shrugging his shoulders. "But I can spare only two men. The rest will have to go about their regular duties."

"We can ask the local police to help," the young sleuth suggested. "Perhaps they can spare a couple of—"

"Out of the question!" the curator declared indignantly. "Policemen attract newspaper reporters. I'm not going to risk wild rumors being circulated that something is wrong here at the museum."

Frank was annoyed by the man's attitude. Watkins was more worried about his personal image than about the protection of the collection.

"Anyway," the curator continued, "you're only acting on a hunch."

"Have it your way," Frank said tartly. "I hope you won't have reason to regret your decision."

"Hardly," Watkins assured him. He grinned. "You detectives tend to be overly suspicious. I doubt if the thieves are within a thousand miles of this museum."

At that moment a tall, muscular, hard-faced

man entered the basement. He was carrying a pair of shears which he placed in a tool chest. Then he hurried away. Something about the man made Frank uneasy.

"Who was that?" he asked the curator in a low voice.

"Our gardener," replied Watkins. "He takes care of the grounds around the building as well as other odd jobs."

"How long has he been employed here?"

"Less than a week, actually. We're lucky to have him. We can't pay very much and it's difficult to find someone to do the work."

The curator added that the man's name was Starker, and that he had excellent references.

After the guards were posted, Watkins invited Frank to his home for dinner.

"Thank you. But I'd better stick around here. I'll have a quick meal at one of the local restaurants later."

As night approached, Frank had the guards help him check all doors and windows. Then he decided to have some food. One of the men recommended an eating place about seven blocks from the museum.

Frank strolled out of the building and down the street. He had not walked very far when he realized that two men were following him.

As he quickened his pace, so did his pursuers. Gradually they gained on him. As the gap between them narrowed, Frank arrived at the restaurant and dashed inside.

"Soup's all gone, and so are the menu specials," a waiter announced as Frank quickly sat down at a table. "We're closing in half an hour."

Frank did not speak. He stared at the door apprehensively. The men did not follow him into the restaurant. Obviously they wanted to avoid being seen, and were waiting for him outside.

"How about a sandwich?" the waiter went on as he glanced at his watch impatiently. "Best I can do."

Frank made a selection and was quickly served. As he ate, he desperately tried to think of a way to escape his pursuers. He finally decided to call the police.

"Where's the telephone?" Frank asked the waiter.

"There's none here in the restaurant," the man replied. "You'll find a public booth on the corner half a block down the street."

"But you must have a phone here somewhere!" the boy insisted.

"Sure," the waiter said icily, eyeing Frank with suspicion. "We have one in the kitchen. It's strictly for business, not for customers."

"This is an emergency! You must let me make a call!"

"Don't give me that," the man snarled. "What's wrong? Too lazy to walk half a block?"

The situation was becoming more desperate. It was now closing time and several of the employees were preparing to leave.

Frank did not like what he was about to do, but he had no choice. "I—I don't think I could walk that far. I feel sick. It—it must've been the sandwich I just ate."

"Just a second, kid," the waiter fumed. "Don't accuse us of serving bad food. All our stuff is the best."

Frank settled into a chair. "Maybe," he groaned. "But I felt fine till now. Ugh—this is awful."

The waiter rushed off and returned with the proprietor of the restaurant.

"What's going on here?" the man demanded. "I hear you don't feel good. I've been in this business twenty years and never poisoned a customer yet!"

"There's always a first time," Frank muttered weakly. "Somebody get me a taxi."

The proprietor turned to the waiter. "Call him a cab," he ordered. "This kid must be some sort of mental case. The sooner we get rid of him the better."

Minutes later a taxi rolled up in front of the restaurant. The owner and several of his employees accompanied Frank as he trudged toward it and climbed in.

"Take me to the museum," he told the driver. As they sped off, he peered out the rear window in time to see two men leap out from a dark alley-way.

Arriving at his destination, Frank went to the basement to check on the storeroom. There the two guards were engaged in idle conversation.

"Everything okay?" Frank asked.

"Yeah," one of the guards replied. "Our only problem is trying to stay awake."

"Whatever you do," Frank warned, "don't fall asleep. I'll get a couple of the other men to relieve you in two hours."

He then hurried to the curator's office to tele-phone his father and report what had happened.

"You had a close call," Mr. Hardy commented. "From what you tell me, I don't think the column fell over by accident, either. And what about the men who followed you?"

"No sign of them," answered Frank. "But I did catch a glimpse of one man. He was tall and mus-cular. I'm sure he was Starker, the museum gar-dener."

"Get help," his father urged. "Call the police in on this. Never mind what the curator said. This could be serious!"

Just then a loud noise echoed through the mu-seum. Frank asked Mr. Hardy to stand by for a moment and quickly placed the phone down on the desk.

"Who's there?" he shouted.

No answer. Frank raced down into the basement. The two guards were on their feet, poised for action.

"We heard a noise!" one of them said excitedly. "What was it?"

Frank was about to reply when his attention was seized by a hissing sound. Then a white, odorless smoke began to filter into the room.

"What's that?" a guard shouted.

In the next instant several men wearing gas masks appeared. Frank lunged at the intruders, but his body seemed to be drained of energy. He fell to the floor, unconscious!

CHAPTER VII

Mysterious Cargo

"WHAT—what happened?" Frank asked groggily as he regained consciousness. He found himself staring into the face of a police sergeant.

"You were knocked out by some kind of gas," the officer replied. "So were all the guards in the building."

Still dazed, Frank struggled to sit up. "But how come you're here?" he inquired. "Who notified you?"

"Your father called headquarters," the sergeant explained. "He said you'd heard a noise in the museum and went to check it out. When you didn't return to the phone, he suspected something was wrong."

Frank glanced around. He saw several policemen inspecting the area. Others were helping to revive the two guards posted at the storeroom door.

Suddenly Frank sprang to his feet. "The De-Graw collection!" he cried. "Is it gone?"

"The storeroom is empty, if that's what you mean," the sergeant replied.

At that instant the curator arrived on the scene. "I received a telephone call to come here at once. What's—?" His words trailed off as he peered into the empty storeroom.

"The collection's been stolen," Frank said.

Watkins's face turned pale. "This is outrageous!" He glared at Frank. "Why didn't you stop the thieves?"

Frank fought hard to control his temper. "I warned you, sir. We should have called in the police."

"Are you trying to blame me for what happened?"

Frank said nothing. He did not want to waste precious time by getting involved in an argument with Watkins. Instead, he began to search the area for clues.

On the floor he spotted a short piece of rope. He examined it closely, then showed it to the police sergeant. "Do you mind if I keep this for a while?" he asked.

The officer looked at it, then returned it to Frank. "We might need it later."

"Certainly."

"I have a couple of men coming over from the crime lab to check for fingerprints," the sergeant went on. "You get some sleep. I'll let you know if we find anything."

"Think I will," Frank agreed wearily. He went to the curator's office and settled down into a comfortable chair.

He slept several hours before he was gently shaken awake. "Hello, son," came his father's voice.

"Dad! When did you get here?"

"A couple of hours ago. I decided to let you sleep a while longer."

Frank grimaced. "Then you know about the robbery."

"It wasn't your fault. I had a talk with the curator. Never met such a stubborn man. He should have given you more cooperation."

Frank filled his father in on all the facts. Then Mr. Hardy said, "We're dealing with a shrewd ring of thieves. But they must know we're on to their game. I have a hunch the gang will wait for a while before they pull off another robbery."

"What's our next move?"

"Breakfast and then back to Bayport. I've already called Joe and the others. The local police have agreed to take over in the other towns and will guard the museums heavily for an indefinite period of time."

Fenton Hardy and Frank arrived in Bayport in the early afternoon. Joe had just come home and was in the study with Chet.

"Hi!" Chet greeted them. "Heard you had a run-in with the museum thieves."

"And they won," Frank replied ruefully.

"By the way," Joe said, "Sam Radley telephoned from California. He had trouble getting an airline reservation and won't be here till tomorrow morning."

At Joe's request, Frank repeated the story about the robbery. Then he produced the piece of rope he had found on the floor of the storeroom.

"Looks like ordinary rope to me," Chet muttered.

"It does," Frank agreed. "My guess is that it's part of the rope the thieves must have used to tie up the loot. But here's what I find particularly interesting. Notice that it's neatly spliced."

Joe shrugged his shoulders. "So what?"

"Doesn't it suggest anything to you?" Frank questioned.

Suddenly Joe's eyes lit up. "Oh, I get it. Experienced sailors are usually good at splicing ropes. Maybe the crew of the *Black Parrot* have been committing the robberies!"

"Could be," said Mr. Hardy. "But I have a hunch that they're only involved in transporting the loot."

Frank agreed. "The thefts seem to be the work of a skilled gang."

Joe eagerly suggested that they try again to investigate the *Black Parrot*. Their father was reluctant. He warned the boys that they would surely be recognized by the captain and most of the crew.

"We won't attempt to board the ship," Frank explained. "We'll observe it from a distance. With luck, we might pick up some useful information."

There was a long pause. "All right, I'll go along with your plan," Mr. Hardy said finally. "But you must be extremely careful."

"We will," Frank promised.

Joe was jubilant. But an instant later his enthusiasm disappeared. "Wait a minute. We've overlooked something. Where do we find the *Black Parrot?*"

"I have a hunch that the ship will be back at the East Coast sooner or later," Frank said. "Let's try all the ports up to Canada."

During the next few days the Hardys checked the shipping schedules in the newspapers, and kept in constant contact with the various harbor authorities. A week went by before Frank's prediction proved to be correct.

"You were right!" Joe said. "The *Black Parrot* is due to dock at Stormwell again day after tomorrow."

"We'll leave for Canada in the morning," Frank decided. "Too bad we can't use Dad's plane. But Jack's flying him to Philadelphia tomorrow. He wants to have another talk with Watkins."

Chet needed no persuading to go along. They arrived at their destination late the following afternoon and checked in at a hotel near Stormwell.

"How about something to eat?" Chet suggested.

"Okay," Frank answered, smiling. "I noticed a dining room just off the lobby."

"So did I," the stout youth admitted.

"You didn't expect Chet to miss any spot where food is served," Joe said to his brother jokingly. "He has a built-in compass that would lead him to all the restaurants within fifty miles."

"Cut it out, fellows," Chet said.

They entered the dining room and sat down at a table. A waiter handed each of them a menu. While they were trying to decide what to order, Frank could not help overhearing a conversation between two men sitting at an adjacent table.

"The *Black Parrot* wasn't due in till tomorrow," one of them said angrily. "So what happens? The ship shows up a couple of hours ago. It's forcing me to rearrange my docking schedule."

"I don't like those *Parrot* ships, anyway," the other man commented. "There's something strange about them. Wish they'd stay away from Stormwell."

"Luckily the *Black Parrot* won't be in port long. It isn't picking up much cargo, and the crew looked as if they were in a big hurry to get underway again."

Frank leaped to his feet. Followed by Joe and

Chet, he rushed past the startled waiter and out of the restaurant.

The hotel manager quickly secured a rental car, and the boys headed for the docks.

As they approached the waterfront, Joe pointed toward the pier. "There she is! What's that they're hauling aboard?"

"Looks like a pile of logs," Chet said. "I'd say about a dozen."

Frank's attention was focused on a flatbed truck from which the cargo was being lifted. On the side of the vehicle was the name *Norland Lumber Company, Cloud Lake, Canada.*

The boys watched as the logs were lowered into the hold of the *Black Parrot.* Then crewmen began to scurry around the deck. Shortly the ship's engines rumbled and a boiling caldron of foamy water appeared at the stern.

"That was a short visit," Chet muttered as he and the Hardys watched the freighter glide away from the pier.

"Odd," Joe remarked. "Why would the ship come here just to pick up a dozen logs?"

Frank's thoughts were elsewhere at the moment. "Norland Lumber Company," he said to himself. "This might be worth investigating."

The boys saw two men climb into the truck and drive off.

"What do you make of it?" Joe asked.

"I'm not sure yet," Frank said. "But right now,

I think we'd better check out that lumber company."

After returning to the hotel, Frank phoned the local police.

"Yes. I can tell you something about the Norland firm," an officer said in response to his question. Actually, it's a lumber mill. I hear it may close down."

"Where is it located?"

"Thirty miles northwest of here—just off the Old Pine Road."

"Thank you," Frank said. He hung up and turned to his companions. "Let's drive out to the mill."

"But it'll be dark when we get there," Joe pointed out.

"I know, but time is important."

They hurried to the car and started off. The Old Pine Road was unpaved and driving was difficult.

Suddenly the car began to wobble. Frank stopped and jumped out. Seconds later he gave a cry of dismay, "We have a flat!"

"Great!" Joe muttered in disgust. "Just what we need!"

He and Chet helped Frank to take out the spare tire. While Frank jacked up the car, Chet flopped down on the spare. *Pffft!* The tire collapsed under his weight.

"Oh, no!" Joe shook his head. "The spare's no good!"

"We're stuck," Frank admitted. He furrowed his brow. "The mill can't be more than a mile from here. Let's walk."

Chet did not think much of this suggestion, but he did not want to stay in the car, either. "I'd better go along," he mumbled. "Somebody has to see to it that you guys don't get into trouble!"

The trio trudged on. Darkness had settled over the trees and progress was slow.

Joe took out his flashlight and scanned the area. "Look," he said. "Tire tracks!"

"They were made by a heavy truck," Frank concluded. "Like the one we saw at the pier."

He motioned Joe and Chet to halt, and listened intently.

"What's the matter?" Joe whispered after a few minutes of tense silence.

"I thought I heard something in the under-brush."

"Like what, for instance?" Chet quavered.

Frank shone his light at the trees, but all was still. "Maybe it was just a squirrel."

"I think we should wait till tomorrow," Chet suggested. "This looks like trouble!"

"Why don't you walk back to the car and Joe and I'll go alone," Frank said.

Chet shifted uncomfortably from one foot to

the other. "No," he said. "I'll come with you."

Proceeding cautiously, they finally spotted a small group of wooden buildings ahead. Light came from a window in one of them.

"That must be the mill," Joe whispered.

Frank nodded, then signaled to his brother and Chet to follow.

All at once the ground gave way beneath them. A split second later the boys plunged into a deep hole!

CHAPTER VIII

Fire!

THE boys lay stunned. Shortly, beams of light pierced the darkness from the rim of the hole above.

"We have visitors," a man's voice snarled.

"Three, to be exact," said another.

"Who are you?" Frank demanded as he struggled to his feet.

There was no response. Instead, a rope was tossed down into the hole.

"Start climbin' out of there!" one of the men ordered. "And don't try anythin'. We're armed."

Frank helped his brother and Chet to their feet. Then they hoisted themselves up out of the hole. The boys could only make out the vague images of three men holding pistols and powerful flashlights.

"Now talk!" one of the men growled. "What're you kids doin' here?"

"Sightseeing," Chet said innocently.

"The fat one's a comedian!" the fellow boomed. "He won't think it's so funny when we throw them back in the hole."

They stepped closer and the tallest of the three stared at Frank and Joe. "I recognize these two!" he shouted. "They were taken off the *Black Parrot* by policemen in Stormwell."

"They're snoopers!" the man to his right exclaimed nervously. "We'd better get outta here. They might be workin' for the police!"

"Okay. But first, let's take these kids to the shack and tie 'em up. We don't want 'em trailin' us."

The Hardys and Chet were herded to one of the wooden structures and shoved inside. Then their arms and legs were tightly bound with ropes. When the job was finished, the three men left. For a few seconds they stood outside talking in the dark.

Joe rolled over and pressed an ear to the wall.

"What'll we do now?" one man whispered.

"Head for Port Manthon. The *Yellow Parrot*'s docked there for repairs," said another. "We'll board it and sail out of the country. Let's get the truck. We can make it in three or four hours if we hurry."

When they moved on, Joe excitedly relayed the conversation.

Frank said, "Port Manthon is about a hundred

miles farther up the coast. If only we could get loose and—" His words were interrupted by the sound of a truck's engine being started.

"They're leaving!" declared Joe.

As the men drove off, a shower of glowing carbon sparks spouted from the vehicle's exhaust pipe. The red-hot particles landed in some dry brush. Smoke appeared, then flames.

Unaware of what was happening, the boys tried to free themselves.

Chet suddenly yelled, "I smell smoke!"

"So do I!" Joe said.

"Fire!" exclaimed Frank.

Outside, the flames were spreading at a furious rate. Soon the boys could feel the heat radiating through the thin, wooden walls of the shack.

"We've got to get out of here!" Joe cried. He rolled across the floor toward the door of the structure and kicked it open. "Come on!" he urged his companions.

Frank and Chet quickly followed. Outside, Joe found the sharp edge of a partially embedded rock and used it to cut the ropes binding him. Then he freed the others.

The boys looked around in horror. They were completely encircled by a raging inferno. The heat was almost unbearable.

"We're done for!" Chet shouted.

"The mill is beginning to catch fire!" Frank cried.

Desperately the Hardys sought some means of escape. There was none!

Then Joe grabbed his brother's arm. "Listen!"

A flapping noise came from the distance. As the sound grew louder, they looked up to see a Royal Canadian Air Force helicopter hovering overhead.

"Wh-what's going on?" Chet stammered weakly.

"We're getting out of here!" Frank shouted to him.

The boys waved their arms wildly. A rescue sling was lowered from the chopper, and, one by one, they were hoisted aboard.

Then the craft hovered over the site of the fire, pouring ribbons of white foam on the blaze. Another helicopter joined it, and together they extinguished the fire.

"We reached you just in time," said one of the crew members. "What were you fellows doing in the middle of a forest fire?"

The Hardys told him what had happened. They said that they were not sure how the fire had started.

"Perhaps one of the men threw a match, either carelessly or intentionally, on the dry brush," Frank concluded.

"Looks that way," the crew member agreed. "Anyway, the glow was sighted all the way from Stormwell. We were asked to help."

After several minutes the helicopter landed on a small airfield well beyond the scene of the fire. Provincial police were on hand when they arrived. The young sleuths identified themselves and repeated their story.

"What you fellows told us fits in with an arrest we made an hour ago," explained one of the officers. "Three men were stopped for speeding outside of Stormwell in a truck. I recognized two of them as being wanted for larceny and fraud. They're already on their way to Montreal for questioning."

Then Frank, Joe, and Chet were driven back to their hotel. They had a quick meal, after which Frank placed a telephone call to his father. Mr. Hardy listened to his sons' adventure with great interest.

"You've really come up with something," he said. "I'll have Jack fly me to Montreal tomorrow. I want to interrogate these three men."

"Meanwhile, we'll go to Port Manthon to check on the *Yellow Parrot*," Frank told his father.

"Good idea," Mr. Hardy replied.

Next morning Frank rented another car and arranged for the first one to be recovered. Then they started off. The trip took a little more than two hours. When they arrived in Port Manthon, they drove along a road looking down onto the water. Frank pulled into a turnoff and parked. Then the boys got out to scan the waterfront.

Joe spotted the *Yellow Parrot* tied to a pier.

"There she is," he said.

Frank nodded. "Port Manthon is not very big. Doesn't appear as if it could accommodate more than two or three ships at a time."

"That might be the reason she came here," his brother said. "More privacy."

The boys observed the freighter for a while. There was a gaping hole in its hull near the bow. Several crewmen were repairing the damage.

"Strangers around here, aren't you?" came a voice from behind them. "Interested in ships?"

They whirled around to see a bewhiskered old man who had walked up quietly behind them.

"Why—er—yes," answered Joe.

"We were just passing through," Frank added, "and stopped to take a look at the port."

"Not much to see these days," the man replied with regret. "Used to be mighty active around here years ago." A smile spread across his face. "But it's always good to meet up with lads who like the sea."

"Not me!" Chet interrupted. "I'm—"

His words were cut off by a sharp nudge of Joe's elbow.

"Are you from this area?" Frank put in quickly.

"Born in Port Manthon, and sailed my first ship from here nearly sixty years ago," the man said proudly. "Name's Falop. Captain Falop."

There was an exchange of handshakes. The

boys gave only their first names. Then Frank pointed toward the *Yellow Parrot* and asked, "What happened to that ship?"

"Don't quite know," Falop answered. "Never saw it in here before. Odd crew. Don't want to talk much. Different from my day." He rubbed his chin dubiously. "I asked one of 'em about the damage. Can't understand why he'd try to get away with such a lie."

"Lie?" Joe echoed. "What do you mean?"

"The fella told me their ship'd run aground," explained the man, "and that the hole was caused by a sharp rock. Nonsense!"

"Why do you say that?" Frank asked.

"The hole's well above the water line and is too neat," Falop replied. "If you ask me, I think it was done by a shell."

"You mean the ship was fired on?" Chet questioned excitedly.

"As far as I'm concerned it was."

"Wonder how long it will take to repair the damage," Frank remarked, trying to act nonchalant.

"I'd say at least two or three days," Falop replied.

The boys continued to watch the activity aboard the *Yellow Parrot*. After a while they said good-by to the captain and checked in at the only hotel in Port Manthon. That evening Frank telephoned the authorities in Montreal and asked if his father had arrived there. A police officer stated that he had, and gave Frank the number of Mr. Hardy's hotel.

When Frank reached him there, his father said, "Hope you had better luck than I did, so far. If those three men know anything about the museum robberies, they're certainly not admitting it. I'm going to try again tomorrow."

Frank then told him about the ship, and what Falop thought had caused the damage to her hull.

"Hm! Very interesting," said Mr. Hardy. "Perhaps I'd better request a complete investigation."

"I've another idea," Frank went on. "If it works, we might learn once and for all if the *Parrot* ships are involved in the case."

"What do you have in mind?"

"Joe and I want to sail aboard the *Yellow Parrot!*"

CHAPTER IX

A Daring Plan

MR. HARDY strongly objected to Frank's plan. "It's too dangerous!" he insisted. "You and Joe have been seen by crew members of the *Black Parrot*. What if some of them switched ships in the meantime?"

"I doubt it, Dad," his son answered. "Their sailing schedules were such that they never came within miles of each other during the past few weeks."

"I still don't like it."

"We'll be careful."

There was a moment of silence. "Okay," Mr. Hardy finally said reluctantly. "But make sure your plan is foolproof before going ahead with it."

"We will," Frank promised.

Chet tingled with excitement as he listened to the plan. "This is going to be fun!" he exclaimed. "I can't wait to get aboard!"

Frank patted him on the shoulder. "Sorry, old friend," he said sympathetically. "No reason why you should risk your neck. You'll have to go back to Bayport."

"What?" the chubby boy shouted. "I'll do nothing of the sort!"

"We know how you feel," Joe said. "But two of us will have a better chance of getting jobs than three."

Chet's pique gradually changed to a feeling of great disappointment. He continued to plead with the Hardys without success.

"Okay, have it your way," he muttered. "When do you want me to leave?"

"After the *Yellow Parrot* sails," Frank replied. "We might come up with some useful information for Dad in the meantime. Then you can give him a report."

Next day they went to the pier and watched the ship from a distance. Repairs were progressing well. Some crewmen were working with acetylene torches, while others were positioning new metal plates over the gaping hole in the hull.

"Looks as if the job is almost finished," Joe observed.

"You're right," Frank agreed. "We'd better start putting our plan into action."

They found a general store in town and purchased work clothes, then returned to the hotel to eat and change.

"We'd better put our plan into action," Frank said

"I hope there's no one from the *Black Parrot* aboard," Joe remarked as he pulled on a denim jacket.

"I'm sure there isn't," Frank said.

Chet listened quietly to their conversation. He grunted a couple of times to let his friends know he was still unhappy about being left out.

Frank and Joe had finished dressing and the three went back to the pier.

"What do you want me to do?" Chet muttered.

"Keep an eye on the ship when we go aboard," Frank instructed. "I don't expect trouble, but it'll be good to know you're around to help—just in case."

Chet could not suppress a slight smile. "You can depend on me."

The Hardys walked toward the *Yellow Parrot* and climbed the gangplank to the main deck.

"What are you fellows doin' aboard?" called out a stocky, tough-looking man.

"We'd like to see the first mate," Joe said.

"What about?"

"Jobs."

The man laughed. "Hey, Rawlin!" he shouted sarcastically. "Here's a couple of old salts wantin' to sign on."

The young detectives turned to see a tall, wiry man march down the deck toward them. "Who are you?" he demanded.

"Frank and Joe . . . Karlsen," Frank replied.

"From around here?"

"No," Joe said. "We've been traveling and doing odd jobs. But what we really want is a chance to go to sea."

Rawlin was hesitant. "I've got to think about it first."

"Why not sign 'em on?" the crewman suggested. "The king can always use a couple of more hands—"

"Shut up!" Rawlin growled.

"King?" asked Frank. "What king?"

"Well—er—I meant the cap'n," stammered the crewman. "Sometimes I call him the king."

Much to their surprise, Frank and Joe were hired and ordered to report the next morning. Elated, they hurried to tell Chet of their success.

"Dad should be home by the time you get to Bayport," Frank told his friend. "Tell him our plan is going well. We'll try to establish contact as soon as we can."

Still disgruntled, Chet departed for home that evening. Early the next day Frank and Joe reported aboard the *Yellow Parrot*. Rawlin was the only one on deck when they arrived.

"So you two were serious about going to sea," he said. "I didn't think you'd be back."

"We wouldn't miss this for anything," Joe replied.

"I'm assigning you to general duties," Rawlin went on. "We'll be sailing in two hours." He shouted through a hatchway. "Evans! Get up here!"

A thin middle-aged man appeared. "Yes, sir?"

"Find a couple of bunks for these two up forward. Then take 'em to the cargo hold with you. Make sure everything's secured."

Evans led the boys down a passageway and into a small cubicle which was to serve as their quarters.

"Not much room," Frank observed.

"Barely enough space to breathe," Joe replied.

"Don't complain," Evans snapped. "There's a lot of things you won't like aboard this ship."

The Hardys exchanged glances. Then they stowed their gear and followed the crewman to the cargo hold.

"Look!" Joe whispered. He pointed to a pile of logs tied down at the far end of the hold. "They're just like the ones we saw hoisted aboard the *Black Parrot*."

"Start checking this stuff!" Evans yelled. "Make sure it's all battened down!"

The boys did as they were told. Gradually, during the course of their inspection, they edged their way toward the pile of logs. Frank began to examine them closely.

"What are you doing?" Evans shouted in annoyance.

"Checking the cargo," Frank answered.

"Then keep moving!"

"You want us to do a good job, don't you?" Joe retorted.

"None of your back talk!" Evans gave Joe a hard shove.

Frank stepped in and the crewman lashed out with his fists. The young detective grabbed his opponent's left wrist, and with a lightning move, pinned the man's arms behind his back.

"Let go of me!" Evans yelled.

"Not unless you calm down."

"Okay! Okay!"

Frank released him. "Now I suppose you're going to report us to the captain."

Evans was embarrassed by having been over-powered. "Naw," he growled. "I'll get even with you two later. Go to your quarters and wait for further orders."

"This should be a pleasant voyage with him around," Joe said, shaking his head.

"We'll just try to stay out of his way," Frank replied. "Trouble is what we don't want."

When they arrived at their quarters, Frank spotted a note on his bunk. He snatched it and a cold chill quivered down his spine as he read aloud:

" *'Get off this ship before it's too late!'* "

CHAPTER X

Deck Watch

"Who could have written this note?" Joe exclaimed.

"I don't get it!" Frank said. "I'm sure none of the crew knows who we are. Yet someone's trying to warn us."

The ship's engines started and the hull vibrated.

"We're getting underway," Joe observed. "That was a pretty quick repair job."

Frank stuffed the note into his pocket. "Too late to worry about this now. We'll have to take our chances."

"You kids!" came Evans's voice. "Get up on deck and help haul in the lines!"

The Hardys hastened topside, where they saw the bow of the *Yellow Parrot* swerving away from the pier.

"Come on! Come on!" Evans barked. "Get working!"

Frank and Joe assisted the other crewmen. Soon the heavy lines were pulled aboard and stacked in neat coils.

The job was hardly finished when Evans began shouting orders again. "Now get below and report to the ship's carpenter. Ask him to give you some paint. There are a few vents around here I want redone."

"We won't have time to do any investigating with him around," Joe said under his breath.

"We'll have to be patient and hope for a break," Frank replied.

The Hardys were kept busy painting. Later that day Joe was high on a ladder daubing the top of a door when his paint can slipped.

Splat! It hit the deck with a thud, spattering a gray mess in all directions.

What was worse, Rawlin walked past the spot at that very moment. He was decorated with gooey blobs.

Enraged, he looked up and shouted at Joe. "Hey, you! Come here!"

Joe quickly climbed down the ladder. Frank, who had been working nearby, ran over to see what had happened.

"What's the meaning of this?" Rawlin roared.

"It was an accident," Joe said.

The man's face reddened. "I don't believe you! I think you saw me coming and dropped that can on purpose. You'll—!"

"Now wait a minute," Frank interrupted.

"Shut up! You stay out of this!" Rawlin shouted. He turned to Joe and grabbed the boy by the lapel of his jacket. "I oughta wipe up the deck with you!"

In a sudden move Joe broke away from the man's grip.

"What's going on here?" a voice boomed.

The boys turned to see a burly man of medium height approaching. He had a large graying mustache and cold blue eyes.

"Hello, Cap'n," Rawlin said. "These two kids just signed on. The blond-haired one almost hit me with a can of paint."

"That true?" the officer demanded as he glared at Joe.

"It was an accident, sir."

"That's what he says," snarled Rawlin. "And what's more, he tried to get tough with me just now."

"Oh, yeah?" the captain growled. "Lacks discipline, eh? A couple of days on bread and water in the brig will take the fight out of him."

Frank pleaded with the men on his brother's behalf. It was useless. Joe was taken to the brig below decks. It was a small enclosure with a door of metal bars. No guards were posted.

Late that night Frank secretly made his way to the ship's galley and collected some food. Then he sneaked quietly to the brig.

"Joe!" he whispered. "I brought some chow."

"Great! I'm starved."

Frank passed the food through the bars and watched as Joe ate heartily. Then they discussed the situation.

"I hate leaving you in there," Frank said. "But if you were to break out, it would only rile the captain further and possibly ruin our chances to investigate the ship."

"Don't worry," Joe replied. "I won't upset the applecart." He forced a grin. "Just keep the food coming every night and I'll be able to put up with anything."

"It should only be for a couple of days," Frank assured him. In the meantime, I'll get our investigation underway."

"What do you plan to do first?"

"Examine those logs we saw in the hold. I've a hunch that's not an ordinary pile of lumber."

"What about the warning note? Any idea who wrote it?"

"No, not yet," Frank admitted. "But if we were recognized by someone aboard this ship, then I think the note was meant to be a friendly warning. Otherwise he would have turned us over to the captain by now."

"If you're right, I wish that that someone

would come out into the open. I don't like having mystery friends for too long."

Frank agreed. "Now I'd better be on my way. See you tomorrow night."

"Good luck."

Frank began to edge his way in the direction of the cargo hold. As he rounded the corner of a passageway, he suddenly found himself face to face with Rawlin.

"What are you roaming around for?" the first mate demanded.

"Well—er—I was just getting acquainted with the layout of the ship," Frank stammered.

"Get back to your quarters!" Rawlin commanded.

Crestfallen, Frank obeyed, but decided that he would try again the following night. He fell into his bunk and was soon asleep. To him, it seemed only seconds later that he was being shaken awake.

"Up on deck!" a hefty crewman yelled.

Frank pulled on his pants and quickly followed the man up the ladder. Dawn was just breaking as Rawlin's voice boomed through the crisp, fresh morning air.

"Everyone's to carry on with his regular duties! Frank Karlsen is to report to me!"

Frank went up to the first mate.

"I'm assigning you to deck watch," Rawlin told

him. "Four hours on, and four hours off. Now report to the bridge."

Frank was bored with his new duty. But what bothered him even more was the fact that he had to remain in one spot and could not wander about to search for information.

It was well after midnight when he was relieved from his third watch of the day. He hurried off and repeated his secret journey to the brig with food for Joe.

"I thought you'd forgotten me, Frank," Joe said jokingly.

"Never, old buddy." Frank told him about his new assignment and his encounter with Rawlin the night before.

"That guy seems to be everywhere at once," Joe remarked. "When do you plan to try again?"

"Now. I noticed a storm to the east when I left watch. Rawlin is on the bridge keeping an eye on it. He won't be back this way tonight."

The ship began to roll gently. "The sea is beginning to get a bit rough," Joe commented.

"I'd better head for the cargo hold," Frank said. "There's no telling how much weather we're in for."

"Be careful," Joe warned. "And if this storm gets too rough, ask the captain to let me out of here."

Frank nodded. As he went down the passageway

toward the cargo hold, he heard the clamor of footsteps ahead and looked around for a place to hide. He spotted the door of a small equipment locker, opened it, and ducked inside.

"Come on! Come on!" a crewman yelled. "Rawlin wants us forward. Looks like we're in for some real weather!"

Frank estimated that about half a dozen men rushed past his hiding place. Fortunately they were headed away from the cargo hold.

He crept out of the locker and reached the cargo hold. By now the intensity of the storm had increased and the ship rolled violently.

Frank took out his flashlight and directed its beam toward the pile of logs. As he did, the ship lurched under the impact of the heavy sea. The logs broke loose from their bindings and came avalanching toward him!

CHAPTER XI

Unknown Ally

LOUD, crashing sounds thundered through the hold as the logs hurtled across the deck.

Frank looked up and spotted a steel girder that spanned the beam of the ship. Making a desperate leap, he grabbed it and swung his body upward. The logs rolled beneath him.

Crash! Bang! They collided with the bulkhead on the portside, then tumbled back across the deck in the opposite direction as the ship listed to starboard. The cycle was repeated again and again —solid thuds with an occasional hollow boom.

As Frank clung to the girder with all his strength, the storm seemed to become even more violent.

"Can't hang on much longer," he said to himself. "But if I let go—"

The lights in the hold were turned on. Several crewmen poured in through the hatchway. For a moment they stared at the logs hurtling back and forth across the deck, then set about tying them down again.

Frank watched as they gradually brought the situation under control. Then he released his grip on the girder and dropped to the floor.

"What are you doin' in here?" shouted one of the men.

At that instant the captain entered the hold. "Everything under control?" he asked.

"Yes, sir. But we were wonderin' what this kid's up to. He was hangin' from that girder when we got here."

The captain glared. "Your place is up forward!"

Frank frantically searched his mind for an explanation. "I'd just gotten off deck watch and couldn't sleep," he said. "So I decided to take a walk."

"In this storm?"

"The weather wasn't too bad when I started out," Frank answered. "Then it got worse. I heard a lot of noise here in the hold and wanted to see what it was."

"Why didn't you call for help when you saw that the logs had broken loose?"

"I was going to, sir," Frank replied. "But when the logs rolled toward me, I jumped for the girder."

The captain rubbed his chin dubiously for a

few seconds. Finally he accepted Frank's explanation and ordered him to return to his quarters.

By daylight the storm had subsided and the *Yellow Parrot* was churning its way through calm waters. Frank was returning from deck watch when he saw his brother walking down the passageway toward him.

"Hi, Joe!" he called out. "When were you sprung from the brig?"

"A few hours ago. But they put me to work right away in the engine room. I'm bushed."

"I don't have to be back on watch till midnight," Frank said. "Let's get some sleep. Then we'll plan our next move."

The boys slept soundly for several hours. After a late lunch in the galley Frank told his brother that he was still determined to examine the logs.

"I'm with you," Joe said. "But you've already been caught there once."

"That's a chance we'll have to take," Frank told him. "Come on."

They edged their way toward the hold and were elated to find no crewmen in the area.

"It's pitch black in here," Joe whispered as the two entered the hold and closed the hatch behind them.

"We don't want to turn on the lights," Frank said. "Use your flashlight."

They directed their beams of light at the pile of logs.

"Funny thing," Frank muttered.

"What's that?"

"I might have just imagined it, but when the logs rolled back and forth across the deck, some of them sounded as if they weren't completely solid. They sounded hollow."

"You mean," Joe began, "that the—" A faint noise caused him to stop abruptly.

"Switch off your light!" Frank hissed.

The boys' pulses quickened as they stood motionless and waited in the darkness. Then they heard the noise again. This time it came from a point directly behind them.

The Hardys whirled around. At the same instant they were blinded by an intensely bright flash of light.

"I'm trying to help you!" a man said. "Stop your investigation. Get off this ship as soon as you can!"

Before either boy could question the man, there was the sound of the hatchway door being slammed shut as he exited from the hole.

"What now?" Joe asked.

"We'd better get out of here," Frank said. "That guy might've been spotted leaving. He could bring someone to check this place out."

The boys hurried to the hatch. They eased open the door, saw that the area was clear, and darted out. Back in their quarters, they discussed what had happened.

"Whoever it was," Joe remarked, "he must be the one who wrote the warning note."

"Without question," his brother replied. He paused for a moment. "But I'd like to know what his game is. If he knows who we are, why is he being so mysterious about it?"

"Could be he's holding out for money," Joe suggested. "I mean, he might be planning to demand payment in exchange for being quiet."

Frank pondered this. "I doubt it. If that was his motive, he certainly would have approached us with a deal by now."

"What's our next move?"

"Let's go on deck and take a walk around the ship. We might come up with a lead."

Strolling along in a nonchalant manner, the Hardys watched as the sailors went about their duties. As they were passing the radio room, Frank suddenly grabbed his brother's arm.

"Listen!" he whispered excitedly.

The door was partially open. Inside, two men were engaged in conversation. One of the voices belonged to the stranger they had encountered in the hold!

"Good grief!" Joe exclaimed in a low tone. "That must be the guy we're after!"

"Looks that way!"

A few seconds later the two men appeared in the doorway, still talking. One of them looked like an ordinary sailor. The other was a lean, red-haired young man with pleasant features. Apparently he was the ship's radio operator. It was his voice the Hardys had identified.

"Okay," the crewman told him. "I'll have the antenna checked right away."

"Good." The young man turned and went into the radio room. Before he could shut the door, the boys dashed in after him.

"Hello," Frank said. "Mind if we have a few words with you?"

There was a pause before the startled operator spoke. His face had turned pale. "You—you want to talk to me? What about?" he stammered.

"What's your name?" Frank asked.

"Clay—Clay Ellis. I'm the ship's radioman."

Joe got straight to the point. "Writing warning notes and creeping around dark cargo holds must be a hobby of yours."

"I—I don't know what you mean," Ellis countered.

Frank, meanwhile, had peered around the room and spotted a camera flash gun on a shelf.

"Is this yours?" he asked, picking up the object.

"Er—no—one of the crew must have left it here," the operator said nervously.

Frank looked closely at the base of the flash gun and noticed the letters C.E. scratched on the metal surface. "This is a coincidence," he commented. "These seem to be your initials."

Perspiration oozed from Ellis's forehead. "All right! It's mine. So what?"

"You took our picture in the cargo hold a little while ago," Joe accused.

The young man let out a deep sigh. "Guess there's no sense in trying to lie to you," he muttered. "I didn't take your photograph, just wanted not to be seen. That's why I blinded you with the flash gun. You see, I know you're the Hardy boys."

ɼ"How did you learn that?" Joe asked.

"I've been interested in crime stories and the work of famous detectives for years," Ellis explained. "Photographs of you and your father have appeared in many publications I've read. I recognized you the minute you boarded the ship."

"Why are you trying to warn us?" Frank questioned impatiently.

"You fellows are here to investigate the *Yellow Parrot,* I'm sure," the operator went on. "But believe me, you've walked into a lion's den. I don't want anything to happen to you."

"We appreciate your concern for our safety," Joe put in sarcastically. "What's your game? Why haven't you reported us to the captain?"

"I—I can't give you my reasons," Ellis said apprehensively.

"Are there any other crew members here who know who we are?" Frank asked.

"I'm sure I'm the only one. But don't worry. Your secret is safe with me."

"Thanks," Frank said. "Isn't there any more you can tell us about yourself, or the *Yellow Parrot?*"

An expression of fear spread across Ellis's face. "I've nothing to say," he insisted. "Anyway, you don't realize what you're getting into. Take my advice and get off this ship just as soon as you can. I'll help you."

"You seem anxious to get rid of us!" Joe stated.

At that instant a sailor entered the room and handed a folded sheet of paper to Ellis. "The cap'n wants you to send this out right away," he announced.

As he hurried off, the operator read the message. Then he walked over to the radio and flicked a switch.

"I'd better start warming up the transmitter," he said. "This message looks important."

"What does it say?" Joe asked quickly.

Ellis gazed at the boys for a moment. Then he handed them the sheet of paper. "You realize that I'm not supposed to do that," he said quietly. "But I trust you."

Frank took the message while Joe looked over his shoulder. After he had finished reading it, he said gravely, "Oh, oh. This could mean real trouble."

Ellis stared at him in surprise. "What's wrong?" he inquired. "It only says that I'm to contact the captain of the *Black Parrot* and arrange for a rendezvous with the ship tomorrow off Tambio Island."

"That's just it," Frank muttered.

CHAPTER XII

Swim to Freedom

NOT without some misgivings on Frank's part, the Hardys took Ellis into their confidence, telling him briefly about their adventure aboard the *Black Parrot*.

The radioman was amazed. "This *does* mean trouble. We're bound to be visited by some of the *Black Parrot*'s crew."

"Maybe we can hide somewhere during the rendezvous," Joe suggested.

"That won't work," Ellis warned. "Any time we put into a port, or get close to a landfall, the captain double-checks to make sure all crew members are accounted for. You'd be missed immediately."

Frank began to pace the floor. "We've got to think of something. There must be a way out of this."

"You'd better go back to your quarters," the

operator urged. "Meanwhile, I'll get this message off to the *Black Parrot*. Meet me in an hour on the main deck, amidships on the portside. I should have more information by then."

The boys left and made their way forward.

"What do you make of Ellis?" Frank asked.

"First impressions can be misleading," admitted Joe, "but I like the fellow and feel we can trust him. Anyhow, we haven't much choice."

"I agree. But if he *is* on our side, why doesn't he tell us more about himself?"

"He is frightened of something. I think he's being forced to sail aboard this ship."

Time passed slowly for the Hardys. Finally an hour went by, and they headed amidships for their meeting with the radioman. He was already waiting when they arrived.

"The situation is worse than I thought," Ellis announced in a low voice. "The *Parrots* are going to exchange a few crew members."

"Good grief!" Joe exclaimed. "We're bound to be recognized."

"Your only chance is to get off this ship at Tambio Island."

"And be marooned?" Frank protested.

"You won't be," Ellis assured them. "I hear there's a hermit, or some kind of nutty guy living on the far side of the island. He's said to be friendly. I'm sure you could stay with him until you flag down a ship."

"That would be taking a long chance," Frank said.

"Your chances are nil if you don't get off this ship," the radioman warned.

"When does the meeting take place?" Frank inquired.

"Tomorrow night."

"Oh, oh." Joe sighed, eyeing his brother. "Something tells me we're in for a swim."

"I don't see any other way out," Frank admitted.

"Good," Ellis put in. "I'll meet you fellows here tomorrow night and help you get away. Make it about ten o'clock. That's when we're scheduled to arrive."

The Hardys were kept busy all the following day, and it was well after dark before they were released from duty.

Ding! Ding! came a tinkling.

"Two bells," Joe said. "It's nine o'clock."

"Only an hour to go," remarked Frank. "Let's try to get a few minutes' rest before we meet Ellis."

The boys were walking to their quarters when the first mate shouted to them. "Hey! You kids! Come here!"

"I wonder what he wants," Joe whispered apprehensively as they obeyed Rawlin's command.

"You two are spending the night in the brig," Rawlin growled.

"Why?" Joe demanded angrily. "What've we done?"

"Shut up!" He summoned four members of the crew. "Take them to the lockup."

The men escorted the Hardys below, secured them in the brig, and hurried off.

"Now we *are* in a spot!" declared Joe. "Do you think Rawlin found out about our plan?"

"I doubt it. He's probably being cautious. He's not sure we can be trusted not to jump ship."

A few minutes later a faint shuffling sounded outside the brig. Frank and Joe made out the vague figure of a man approaching.

"Frank! Joe!" Clay Ellis whispered.

The boys sighed in relief.

"I saw what happened," Ellis went on. He produced a small crowbar. "I'll have you out in a jiffy."

The radioman pried away at the door, and it finally sprang open.

"Follow me," Ellis ordered. "The meeting is working out slightly ahead of schedule. We're about a quarter of a mile off Tambio Island."

"Clay—thanks a lot," Frank murmured.

"Any time."

Ellis led the Hardys up on deck and to their previous meeting point amidships. At that instant the *Yellow Parrot*'s engines stopped.

A shout came from the bridge. "Let go the anchor!"

There was a clatter of heavy chains, followed by a loud splash as the anchor plunged into the water.

"You'll have to swim for it," Ellis said. "The shore isn't far off. Think you can make it?"

"Easily," Joe said.

Ellis pointed to a coil of rope he had stowed near the rail. "It will be better if you lower yourselves into the water. If you dive overboard, the crew might hear you."

Frank nodded. "We appreciate all you're doing for us and won't forget it. But I think you're in some kind of trouble."

"You don't seem to belong aboard this ship any more than we do," Joe put in. "Why don't you come with us?"

"I—I can't," the radioman stammered.

Frank pulled a pencil from his pocket and scribbled something on a scrap of paper. He handed it to Ellis. "We have a radio setup in Bayport. Can you transmit on this short-wave frequency?"

"Yes," Ellis replied. "Why?"

"We'll listen in every evening from seven to midnight," Frank told him. "If you should need help or want to give us any information about the activity of the *Parrots,* will you promise to contact us?"

Ellis hesitated for a moment. "I—I promise," he muttered finally.

The Hardys removed their shoes, tied the laces together, and hung them around their necks. Then they knotted one end of the rope around the railing and fed the balance over the side.

"Good luck!" Ellis said in a hushed voice as Frank and Joe quietly lowered themselves into the water.

They waved in response, then began swimming toward the island. In less than half an hour they were trudging up onto a sandy beach.

"Well, we made it," Joe said triumphantly.

Frank gazed silently at his surroundings. The island was covered with trees and thick brush. Finding a couple of fallen branches, he handed Joe one of them. "We'd better start erasing our tracks. Otherwise they'll stand out like road signs when daylight comes."

When the job was finished, the boys walked into the brush and found a clear spot where they could rest. It was not long before they were sound asleep.

Morning was ushered in by a bright, hot sun. The boys woke up to the sound of chirping birds and the rustling of palm trees stirred by an offshore breeze.

Then they became aware of another sound. Men's voices!

"Hear that?" Joe whispered excitedly.

Frank nodded. Stealthily they crawled toward the edge of the brush. On the shore they spotted a dinghy. Several men were scattered along the beach nearby.

"I don't see any sign of 'em!" one of them said to his companions. "No tracks, either. I doubt that they came ashore. They're probably hidin' on the *Parrot* somewhere."

"Yeah!" said another. "Rawlin worries too much. So the kids escaped from the brig. Who cares? And even if they did make it here to the island, what's the difference? They can't cause us any trouble."

"I'm hungry!" exclaimed another man. "We had to miss breakfast because of those brats. Let's go back and get some chow."

The crewmen piled into the dinghy and began rowing toward the *Yellow Parrot*. Frank and Joe looked out to see its sister ship the *Black Parrot* anchored a short distance away.

"Those guys must've been looking for us while we were still asleep," Joe said.

"Lucky you don't snore," Frank quipped.

Eager to locate the hermit, they immediately started trekking easterly across the island.

"Shouldn't take us too long," Joe stated. "Tambio doesn't seem to be very big."

But the thick brush made the going extremely rough. More than three hours passed before they came to the opposite shore. Barely five hundred yards away stood a crude hut, set well back from the high-water mark.

It looked no larger than four by four feet and its door was of sturdy oak.

"What do you think of that?" Joe asked as they came closer.

"It's strange, all right," Frank admitted.

"Should we call out?"

"No, we'd better not. If we startle the guy, he might react violently, especially if he's some kind of unstable recluse."

Frank and Joe walked cautiously around the hut. To their surprise, it had no windows.

"There's no sign of a human being here any-where," Frank remarked.

"Maybe our hermit left a long time ago."

Frank stopped short in his tracks. "Look, Joe, footprints," he said, pointing to the sandy soil partly covered with tufts of coarse grass.

Joe bent over. "They're headed toward the beach. Maybe the fellow's out fishing!"

Frank grinned. "In that case, perhaps we could peek inside." He took hold of the door handle and pulled. It did not budge.

"Here, Joe, give me a hand!"

Joe grabbed the handle, too, and they both tugged. With a creaking noise, the door came open. It took a few seconds for the boys' eyes to adjust to the dim interior. There was nothing but a flight of steep stairs leading into the ground.

"Hey! What's this?" Joe asked.

"Come on. We'll find out."

With Frank in the lead, they carefully descended ten stairs until they came to another door.

Frank knocked gingerly. No one replied.

"Let's go in," Joe whispered.

Frank nodded and opened the door. At the same instant, lights went on in a large room. The boys gasped!

CHAPTER XIII

Trouble on Tambio

On the far side of the room sat a man in a huge high-backed chair. He did not move, did not even bat an eyelash.

"Hello!" Joe blurted out. There was no reply.

Joe looked at Frank. "Is he for real?"

Frank shrugged, and they walked closer.

There was a frozen grin on the man's ebony face and he did not seem to breathe at all. He was attired in a red-and-white-checkered sport shirt, ragged slacks cut off at the knees, and white tennis shoes.

"Wow!" Frank whispered. "He must be right out of Madame Tussaud's Wax Museum!" He stepped forward and touched the man's face. The next moment he yelled, "Joe! He's alive!"

"Of course," said the man. "What made you think I was not?" The grin disappeared from his face and suddenly he looked menacing.

Despite their usual coolness and presence of mind, the Hardys shrank back before the recluse.

"Please do not break into my home again," he said.

With that, a trap door sprang open and the boys were dropped into a shallow pit. Half stunned, they were set upon by the powerful hermit, who sprang at them like a cat. He tied their hands with a piece of rope which he pulled out of his pocket, then brought them back into the room.

It was filled with all sorts of modern appliances. There was an electric stove, a refrigerator, ventilation system and many other devices.

After he had tied the boys by one wrist to sturdy oaken chairs, their captor said, "You are impressed with my home, yes? Perhaps you are wondering how I receive the electrical power for all my treasures? Well, there is an underground generator located just behind the hut."

"Why are you holding us prisoner?" Joe asked.

"As a precaution. First let me ask what you are doing on this island," the man countered.

The Hardys did not want to tell him that they had escaped from the *Yellow Parrot*. There was a possibility, after all, that he was connected somehow with the ship.

"Er—we were sailing our ketch on a long voyage," Frank replied. "A storm came up, blew us

A trap door sprang open and the boys were dropped into a pit!

off course, and finally shipwrecked us not far from here."

\"Ah, I see," the man said. "My name is Katu."

The Hardys introduced themselves by their aliases, Frank and Joe Karlsen.

"It is not often that I have guests," Katu went on. "I am about to prepare lunch. Will you eat with me?"

Eagerly the boys accepted his invitation. They watched with mixed feelings of surprise and amusement as Katu took a package of hamburgers from the freezing compartment of his refrigerator, then switched on the electric stove.

Joe was overwhelmed with curiosity. "How did you come by all these gadgets?" he asked.

"That is not for you to know," Katu answered, displaying annoyance.

He avoided further conversation during the meal. When he finally spoke, it was to announce that they would remain prisoners until his amphibious friend returned.

"Amphibious friend?" Frank repeated. "What do you mean?"

"He flies a plane that can float on the water like a boat," Katu explained proudly, "or roll on the land with wheels."

"An amphibian aircraft!" Frank exclaimed. "It comes here to the island?"

A blank expression spread over Katu's face. He

looked as if he had unintentionally revealed some deep, dark secret.

Before Frank and Joe could ask any more questions, they heard an airplane overhead. It passed low, then seemed to turn toward the sea. Katu left in a hurry.

"Must be the amphibian he told us about," Joe declared.

Frank sighed. "I sure hope he'll let us out of here!"

Twenty minutes later the door to the room opened. A tall, wiry man with sandy-colored hair entered. He was wearing coveralls and leather flight boots.

"Hello," he said, smiling broadly. "My name's Dan Tiller. Katu tells me you fellows were shipwrecked."

The boys nodded. "You must be the pilot of the amphibian," Joe put in.

"That's right," said Tiller. "And who are you?"

Frank and Joe introduced themselves. On a hunch they decided to play it straight and did not use their aliases.

The pilot's eyes widened in surprise. "Are you the sons of Fenton Hardy, the famous detective?"

"Yes," Frank replied. "But—"

"Say!" Tiller interrupted. "I've heard lots about the Hardys. An airline friend of mine met you and your father once. It was on one of his flights that you caught a couple of smugglers aboard the plane."

"Oh, yes. I seem to remember that," Frank muttered, hoping to avoid a lengthy discussion of the case.

"Sorry about the way you were treated. Katu was being a bit overcautious," Tiller said as he loosened their bonds. There was a worried expression on his face.

"Were you fellows really shipwrecked?" he asked. "Or did you come to Tambio to investigate me?"

"Investigate you?" Joe asked curiously. "Why? Have you done anything wrong?"

"No. At least I don't think so. But I don't pay any real-estate taxes." Tiller explained that two years before he had been caught in a storm and was blown off course. When the weather finally cleared, he had spotted a capsized dugout canoe below him. A man was clinging to the craft.

"I landed the amphibian to rescue the fellow," he continued. "It was Katu. I flew him back to my base on Cambrian Island, which is about six hundred miles north of here."

"I've heard of it," Joe interjected. "It's become a popular place for tourists, and its capital is one of the most modern cities in the world."

"Right. Katu liked it there and stayed for a year and a half. He went to school, learned English, and worked in a hotel. We became great friends and flew a lot. One day we discovered this island and decided to make it our Shangri-la, some place where we could get away from the world. It's pretty good, don't you think?"

"Terrific!" Joe said.

"But I don't know if this land belongs to anyone. This underground complex was already here, you see. We might be trespassing on someone's property. But I thought as long as we're not being chased off, it's ours."

"I don't believe you'll have any trouble," Frank assured him.

Now Katu joined them. He grinned as the Hardys praised him for his tricky defense of Tiller's hideout.

The boys took a liking to the pilot and decided to tell him about their escape from the *Yellow Parrot*.

He listened to their story with great interest. "I've never heard of the *Parrots* before," he said. "Ships are a bit out of my line."

"There's something fishy going on with those two," Joe told him. "They're anchored near the west side of Tambio right now."

"How soon will you be flying back to Cambrian?" Frank asked.

"This afternoon."

"Will you take us with you?"

"Of course. From there you can get one of the scheduled flights to Florida."

The Hardys talked a while longer to Tiller and Katu, until the pilot finally said, "Come on, fellows. I want to make it back before dark."

Katu paddled them out to the amphibian, and waved good-by.

"All aboard!" Tiller cried as he led the young detectives through a small hatchway and into the cabin of the plane.

Then he climbed into the cockpit and started the first of the craft's two engines. When it was running smoothly, he fired up the second.

"Here we go!" he shouted and eased the throttles forward. The idling engines erupted into a loud steady roar. The plane bounced across the water and then lifted gracefully into the air.

I As the amphibian gained altitude, Frank dashed into the cockpit. "I know you're in a hurry to get back to Cambrian," he said to Tiller, "but I just had an idea. Would you fly to the other side of the island? We'd like to see if the *Parrots* are still there."

"Sure," Tiller answered as he turned the plane to a westerly heading.

Soon they had reached the coast. A look of disappointment spread over Frank's face when he saw that the ships were gone.

"Too bad," he mumbled. "I thought we might pick up some kind of clue."

"Wait a minute," Joe exclaimed, and pointed

to an object in the distance. "That looks like a ship over there!"

Tiller swung to the direction Joe had indicated. As the distance closed, Frank shouted, "It's the *Yellow Parrot!*"

As they started to circle the ship, thin trails of smoke streaked past the aircraft.

"Tracers!" Joe cried out. "They're shooting at us!"

An instant later a column of thick black smoke began to stream from the plane's left engine!

CHAPTER XIV

Morton's Geyser

"FIRE!" Frank exclaimed.

Tiller turned the plane sharply away from the *Yellow Parrot*. Then he pulled a knob marked "Extinguisher." Immediately faint trails of frozen carbon dioxide streamed from beneath the engine cowling. The boys were relieved to see the black smoke gradually disappear.

"Are you going back to Tambio?" Joe asked.

"No!" replied Tiller. "We can make it to Cambrian on one engine. However, it'll take longer than usual because our speed is reduced."

Hours ticked by. The young detectives were dozing off when Tiller leaned forward for a closer look at one of the instruments on the panel.

"Oh, oh," he muttered. "The right engine's starting to overheat."

"Is it serious?" Joe inquired anxiously.

"Not yet," the pilot answered. "But I'll have to reduce the power setting slightly."

As he eased back on the throttle, the amphibian gradually began to lose altitude.

"We're going down," Frank observed nervously.

"I'll let the plane settle," Tiller decided. "The air is thicker below. It will help to develop a bit more power and lift. Also, we're getting lighter every minute as the fuel burns off."

This statement was of little consolation to the Hardys. They watched the altimeter slowly unwind. Then, at 1,000 feet, the plane acquired new life. The instruments no longer indicated a descent and the engine was now operating at normal temperature.

"Whew!" Joe sighed. "For a while I thought we were going to have to paddle the rest of the way."

"We can relax," Tiller remarked with a wide grin. "The worst is over. I estimate we'll reach Cambrian in about another hour."

It was dark by the time the island came into view. The lights of its capital city twinkled like a small cluster of stars on the horizon.

"I'll use the wheels and land at the airport rather than set down on the water," announced the pilot. He contacted the control tower and was cleared for a straight-in approach.

The landing was smooth, and after parking the aircraft, Tiller obtained a ladder. He climbed up to the left engine, removed the outer cowling, and inspected the damage.

"We're awfully sorry about what happened," Frank said apologetically. "It's our fault and we'd like to pay for repairs."

"Don't worry about it," said the pilot. "As far as I can see, we received one hit in the crankcase. Oil was being splashed over the engine. That's what caused the smoke."

Tiller escorted the boys to the airport terminal building. There they were told that a shuttle flight to Miami would be departing within the hour. After a quick bite to eat, Frank and Joe bid their new friend good-by and took off on the first leg of their journey back home.

They stayed overnight in Miami and arrived in Bayport the following afternoon. Aunt Gertrude let out a cry of surprise when they entered the house.

"Mercy! It's been days and days since we've had any word from you!" she exclaimed. "Where were you? Chasing after some awful criminals, I sup- pose."

The commotion brought Mr. and Mrs. Hardy to the living room. The boys' mother gave them affectionate hugs and Mr. Hardy greeted them warmly.

"You've had me worried," he said. "I was going to notify the authorities and request a search."

An early dinner was prepared while the boys

showered and changed their clothes. During the meal they described their adventures aboard the *Yellow Parrot*.

"You placed yourselves in a very dangerous position," Mr. Hardy remarked with concern. "I'm thankful you decided to escape."

"And, Fenton," Aunt Gertrude interjected, "you should also tell them not to go running off for days at a stretch without letting us know where they are. Even a postcard would be of some consolation."

"Sorry," Joe quipped, winking at his brother. "There wasn't postal service where we were."

"The situation *was* sort of grim," Frank admitted to his father. "And, the worst of it all is that we didn't come up with any real evidence to link the *Parrots* with the robberies."

"But I wouldn't say our trip was a complete loss," Joe said. "Remember, we do have a possible contact in Ellis. He might still change his mind and tell us what he knows."

The boys talked to their father about the tentative arrangement they had made with the radioman.

"We'll have to set up a listening watch," commented Mr. Hardy. "Count on me to do my share. I'll stand by the radio tonight. You two get some rest."

"I'll take my turn tomorrow night," Joe volunteered.

"And we can get Chet to pitch in," suggested Frank.

The brothers retired early and slept until late the following morning. After breakfast they drove to the Morton farm to see Chet.

They were startled to see a geyser of water spouting thirty or forty feet into the air near Chet's home. A police car and an emergency truck were parked nearby.

"What's going on?" Joe exclaimed as they leaped from their convertible. They were met by Iola Morton, a slim, pretty, dark-haired girl. She was Chet's sister and a favorite date of Joe's.

"I'm so happy to see you two!" she cried out. "Isn't this terrible?"

"What happened?" Frank asked quickly.

"Chet became interested in archaeology," explained Iola. "This morning he said that he was on the brink of a great discovery and began digging with a pick. I'm afraid he struck a water main!"

"Oh, no!" Joe shouted.

The boys ran to the scene. There they saw Chief Collig of the Bayport Police Department, a close friend of the Hardys. He was standing transfixed at the sight of the column of water as it gushed upwards.

"Hello, Frank and Joe. Well, your buddy really did it this time. Lucky for him that his parents are visiting friends in Clayton today."

"Where *is* Chet?" Joe asked.

"On the other side of the geyser," Collig replied.

Frank and Joe edged their way around and looked down into the deep hole that Chet had dug. He was kneeling near the water main at the point where it had punctured, and was trying to stcp the flow with his hands.

"Chet! Get out of there!" Joe yelled. "You can't stop it that way!"

Their friend looked up with a startled expression. Then he scrambled out of the hole, dripping wet.

"Hi, fellows," he said, embarrassed. "When did you get back?"

"Never mind that," Frank answered. "What's the archaeological discovery you were digging for?"

Chet glanced about sheepishly. "I—I read that there are lots of old Indian artifacts in our area. I was on the brink of finding something that would've astounded the scientific world."

"Cheer up. You might still have accomplished something," Joe said jokingly. "If that leak isn't fixed soon, you'll have created one of the greatest tourist attractions in Bayport."

"Right," Frank added. "Morton's Perpetual Geyser!"

"Aw, cut it out," Chet said.

At that instant a truck from the water department rolled to a stop. The driver leaped from his vehicle.

"We're shutting the water off at the main junction!" he shouted to Chief Collig.

Then he walked toward the boys. "Which one of you is Chet Morton?"

"Well—er—I guess that's me," Chet stammered nervously.

"I understand you're responsible for this. What were you doing? Digging for gold? Or trying to sabotage the water company?"

"It was an accident," Frank interrupted.

"Just wait till his father gets the bill for repairs," the man went on. "This kid will look like an accident!"

"There goes your allowance for the next two years," Joe needled.

Dejected, Chet strolled slowly to the house and sat down on the porch steps. The Hardys felt sorry for him and followed.

"Don't take it so hard," Frank said sympathetically. "Things could be worse."

"That's what you think," Chet countered.

"Snap out of it," Joe urged. "We're going to need your help."

Chet appeared to perk up a bit. "What kind of help?"

The young detectives told him about their arrangement with Ellis aboard the *Yellow Parrot*.

"You can count on me!" their chum declared.

Then he hesitated. "That is, you'd better wait until my parents come home tonight. I don't know how my father will take the water-main business. He might not give me permission."

"Well, I'm sure he will," Joe said. "This is an important assignment."

The Hardys returned home. After dinner they had just sat down to read the evening newspaper when the telephone rang. Frank answered.

"I'm off the hook!" Chet said jubilantly. The water company found several defects in the pipe I punctured. They said they would have had to make repairs soon, anyway."

"That *is* good news!"

"I've a good mind to charge them for services rendered," Chet went on. "After all, I did part of the work for them by digging the hole."

"If I were you," Frank advised, "I'd leave well enough alone."

"Okay. How soon do I begin my assignment?" Chet inquired eagerly.

"We'll let you know."

Frank hung up and rejoined his brother. Later Mr. Hardy came bounding down the stairs from the study.

"I just received a phone call!" he exclaimed. "Another museum has been robbed of its DeGraw collection!"

CHAPTER XV

Impostors

"WHERE?" Frank asked excitedly.

"The Shillman Museum in Connecticut," his father answered. "Mr. Sedley, the curator, said the guards were knocked out by some kind of gas."

"Again! Just like in Philadelphia," Frank put in.

"Right. I'll have to leave at once. I'd like at least one of you to come with me."

Joe turned to Frank. "You go," he said. "I'll stay here. It's my night to stand radio watch."

Jack Wayne was notified to have the plane ready at the airport. Soon the pilot and his two passengers were airborne.

It took less than an hour to reach their destination. When they landed, Frank and his father took a taxi directly to the museum.

"The alarm system failed to work, yet it showed no signs of having been tampered with," Mr. Hardy explained on the way.

When they arrived at the museum, there were no patrol cars or policemen in the area.

"This is odd," remarked Mr. Hardy. "If a major robbery took place here less than two hours ago, where are the police?"

"Strange," Frank agreed. "But there must be an explanation. At least the curator must be here. He's probably inside waiting for us."

Father and son pounded on one of the large metal doors at the front entrance of the museum. Minutes went by before a door was eased open and an elderly guard peered out.

"What do you want? The museum closes at five o'clock," he said testily. "Come back tomorrow!"

"I received an urgent telephone call from the curator," Mr. Hardy said. "We're here to see him."

"The curator? Mr. Sedley?" the guard replied, eyeing the Hardys suspiciously. "He went home shortly after we closed for the day. Who are you?"

The detective produced his credentials. Suddenly the guard straightened his cap and gave an informal salute. "Mr. Hardy!" he exclaimed. "I've heard of you. I'm Jeremy Turner, chief of the night guards. What can I do for you?"

Bewildered, Frank stared at the man. "Wasn't there a robbery here a couple of hours ago, Mr. Turner?"

"A robbery?" the guard queried with a look of astonishment. "Is this some kind of a joke?"

"I assure you it is not," Mr. Hardy answered impatiently. "I'll have to call Mr. Sedley at once! Take me to a telephone!"

Turner quickly led the detectives to one of the museum's offices. There Mr. Hardy pulled a notebook from his pocket, opened it to a list of telephone numbers, and began to dial. Seconds later he had the curator on the line.

"You say I called about a robbery at our museum?" Mr. Sedley said, after hearing the story. "Preposterous! I did no such thing!"

"That's all I need to know," the detective replied. "Forgive me for being abrupt, but I must leave right away."

He put the phone down, then picked it up again and dialed another number.

"What's up, Dad?"

"I'm calling home," his father told him. "I want to talk to your brother."

Joe answered the telephone. "Hi, Dad," he said. "What about the robbery? Did you—?"

"There wasn't any!" Mr. Hardy quickly told Joe what had happened. "Here's what I want you to do," he went on. "Call the other museums that still have their DeGraw collections and warn them. Frank and I are flying back to Bayport right away."

"Okay, Dad. Will do."

Frank and his father hurried back to the airport. When they landed at Bayport, Joe came running toward them as Jack taxied the plane to the parking ramp.

"Dad!" he cried. "We're too late! The State Museum in Delaware was robbed of their collection around ten-thirty!"

Frank cried out in dismay.

"I was afraid of this," Mr. Hardy said angrily. "As soon as I learned the call from Mr. Sedley was a phony, I suspected it was a trick to draw us away."

He turned to the pilot. "We've got to fly to Delaware right away. While you refuel the ship, I'll check with the curator and the police down there. One wild-goose chase is enough."

"Sure, Mr. Hardy."

The detective rushed off to a telephone. Minutes later he returned. "This time it's the real thing!"

"May I go along?" asked Joe. "Chet's at our house standing by the radio."

"Climb in," his father replied.

The sleek Hardy plane streaked down the Bayport runway on take-off for the second time that night. After an hour plus a few minutes they landed at their destination and headed for the State Museum.

There they found the building swarming with uniformed police and plainclothesmen. As the trio walked inside, a tall, neatly dressed man blocked their way.

"Sorry," he announced. "Only the police are allowed in here."

Mr. Hardy presented his credentials and introduced his sons. A broad smile appeared on the man's face. "This *is* a pleasure," he said. "Never thought I'd have an opportunity to meet you. I'm Seth Spencer, chief of detectives."

There was an exchange of handshakes, then Frank spoke up. "Have you uncovered any leads?"

"Not yet. The thieves seem to have made a clean getaway."

"What about the guards?" Mr. Hardy queried.

"All were knocked out. Since gas was used in the other robberies, they wore masks. But every single mask was punctured!"

"Was the alarm tampered with?"

Spencer rubbed his chin dubiously, "No," he replied finally. "And that's something I can't figure out."

"Were there any eyewitnesses?" Joe asked.

"None who saw the robbery being committed," the officer replied.

"Who notified the police?" Mr. Hardy inquired.

"A passer-by became suspicious when he spotted a trailer-truck race out of the museum driveway with its lights off," Spencer explained, "so he called headquarters. Unfortunately he was unable to give us the license-plate number or a detailed description of the vehicle."

"One thing is certain," Joe remarked. "It was carrying the stolen DeGraw collection."

"Our men and the State Police are checking all trailer-trucks leaving the area," the detective chief said.

After the museum and police officials had completed their investigation, Spencer and the Hardys questioned the guards.

"That's all any of us remember," one of the guards declared. "There was what seemed to be a cloud of gas, and then—"

"By the way, how is Mr. Fosten?" another asked. "Is he all right?"

Spencer looked at the man quizzically. "Mr. Fosten, the curator?"

"Yes, of course."

"My men have been trying to reach him since we learned about the robbery. He's not home and none of his friends know where he is at the moment."

The guard seemed surprised. "He was in his office last time I saw him," he said. "That was right before the robbery. He came back here about an hour after we closed for the day. Said he was going to spend the evening catching up on some paperwork."

"Good night!" Spencer shouted. He summoned his men. "I want you to go through this place again with a fine-toothed comb. Mr. Fosten might be lying unconscious in the building somewhere!"

A thorough search, however, revealed nothing. The detective chief scratched his head in bewilderment.

"Maybe the thieves took the curator along with them," Frank suggested.

"If so," Spencer said, "they'll have a kidnapping charge added to their crime."

Nearly an hour had passed when the telephone rang in the curator's office. A policeman scooped it up, then shouted to Spencer, "You'd better take this call, Chief!"

"I'm Avery Fosten," a voice crackled from the receiver. "Just heard a TV newscast saying the museum was robbed. What's going on?"

"Where are you?" Spencer demanded. "We've been trying to reach you for hours!"

"My wife and I are spending a couple of days at a friend's summer home in Maryland," the curator replied.

"How long have you been there?"

"Since about seven o'clock. The drive took less than two hours."

"But one of the guards here told us he'd seen you working in your office up until the time of the robbery," Spencer said.

"That's absurd!" the curator insisted. "My wife and I left immediately after the museum closed."

"You'd better come back right away. There's something fishy going on here."

After hanging up, Spencer told the Hardys about Fosten's call.

"If he's telling the truth," Frank put in, "there's only one explanation. The man the guard reported seeing in the curator's office was an impostor!"

"You're right," his father agreed. "And a clever plan, too. Disguised as the curator, the impostor had no trouble entering the building after hours. Then he was free to let his cohorts inside without attracting attention."

At that moment a patrolman rushed up to Spencer. "Sir, a trailer-truck was found abandoned on a side road twelve miles north of here," he said. "The crime lab has been checking for fingerprints and other clues. So far they've uncovered nothing."

Frank turned to the detective chief. "Would you issue an alert requesting a check of any flatbed trucks carrying logs?" he asked.

Spencer was a bit puzzled. "Sure—I can do that. But why a truck carrying logs?"

"I can't explain now," Frank replied. "It's only a hunch of mine and may not amount to anything."

Shrugging his shoulders, Spencer walked to a telephone, called headquarters, and ordered a general alert.

Exhausted, the Hardys went to the curator's

office and settled down into comfortable chairs. Soon they were asleep.

It was nearly dawn when a policeman awakened them. "Chief Spencer is back at headquarters," he said. "He just called. The State Police in New Hampshire stopped a flatbed truck hauling logs outside the town of Newland. It was headed north. They checked and found that the license plates were phonies."

"Where's the truck now?" Frank asked quickly.

"At the police garage in Newland. They're also holding the driver and another man who was with him."

The Hardys were driven to the airport in a patrol car. They found Jack Wayne sleeping soundly on a sofa in the operations room.

"Jack!" Frank said as he gently shook the pilot awake. "We've got to fly to Newland, New Hampshire, right away. Is there a field nearby?"

"New-Newland, New Hampshire," Jack murmured as he rubbed his eyes wearily. "I'll check my chart."

He unfolded a map and examined it. There was a small airport located two miles north of the town.

"I'll call the police in Newland and ask if they can have one of their men pick us up at the field," Mr. Hardy said. "How long will it take to get there?"

Jack measured the distance and made a quick

mental calculation. "Approximately two hours."

They had a quick breakfast at the airport before taking off.

When they landed, a uniformed policeman was waiting for them. He led the Hardys to a patrol car and drove to Newland Police Headquarters.

There they were shown the flatbed truck. About a dozen huge logs were piled aboard it.

Frank stared for a moment, then picked up a large stone and walked toward the vehicle.

"What are you up to?" Joe asked.

"If my hunch is correct," his brother replied, "you'll see in a minute!"

CHAPTER XVI

An Unfortunate Scoop

FRANK began to hammer away at each of the logs in turn. Suddenly he struck one that gave off a slightly hollow sound. Then he found another, and another.

"They're not solid!" exclaimed Mr. Hardy.

After close examination Frank gripped the end of one of the logs and began twisting it.

"Give me a hand!" he said to Joe.

Together, they worked on the log. Presently its butt started to turn like a threaded bottle cap. Soon it dropped free.

"Good grief!" Joe cried. "It *is* hollow!"

"Exactly."

Mr. Hardy looked on in amazement as his sons reached inside the log and pulled out crowns, orbs, and several jeweled scepters. Labels on the items proved they were from the DeGraw collection.

"Now we know," Frank said excitedly, "how the thieves transported their loot right under the very noses of the authorities."

"Congratulations!" his father interjected. "Your hunch has solved one aspect of the case."

Arrangements were made to place the truck and its cargo under strict guard. Then the Hardys asked to see the driver and his companion. The policeman who had picked them up at the airport led them into the interrogation room, and the prisoners were brought in.

The driver, who gave his name as Gaff Parkins, was a stocky, tough-looking man. The second man identified himself only as Miker. He was tall, lean, and the deep lines on his face emphasized his hard features. The men were asked if they wanted a lawyer, but both shook their heads.

"Why are we bein' locked up in a cell?" Parkins demanded. "We don't know anythin' about bad license plates. We're just a couple of hired hands."

"Yeah!" Miker added. "Tell us what the fine is and we'll get outta' here."

"You're involved in more than just a motor-vehicle violation," Mr. Hardy informed the prisoners.

"What do you mean?" snarled Parkins. "We ain't done nothin'."

"Except help to rob the State Museum!" Joe snapped.

"I don't know what you're talking about!" Miker declared. "We didn't steal anything. Our job is to haul logs."

"Filled with stolen loot?" Frank put in.

The prisoners glanced at each other with startled expressions.

"I knew there was more to this than we were told," Miker addressed his companion nervously.

"Shut up!"

"I won't!" Miker exclaimed in defiance. "This sounds like big trouble, and we're caught in the middle. Before we get in any deeper, I'm for telling what we know."

Parkins settled back in his chair and sighed. "Maybe you're right," he said.

"Understand," Mr. Hardy told him, "you're not being asked to give a confession. But if you help us, it'll go in your favor."

"Okay," Miker agreed. "A little over a year ago Gaff and I tried to break into the freight-hauling business. Money was a problem, and the only thing we could afford was one flatbed truck."

He went on to explain that recently they ran out of funds and were unable to renew their vehicle registration and to pay for other annual fees necessary to operate the truck.

"Then late yesterday afternoon we got a call from a stranger," Miker continued. "He asked if we could pick up a pile of logs that had been shipped to Wilmington. The money he offered would've put us back in business for at least a year."

"Didn't that make you suspicious?" Frank questioned.

"I was too excited to think straight," the man answered. "He offered to pay us half in advance. But then I remembered we couldn't legally run the truck. I asked the stranger if he could wait a day or two so that I could clear up the matter. He said not to worry, he would give us a special set of Canadian license plates that would get us through."

"I didn't like the whole thing from the start," Parkins put in. "But the guy said the job had to be done that night, or the deal was off."

"Finally we decided to take a chance because the money was just too good to turn down," Miker added. "So we picked up the logs at a dock in Wilmington."

"Where were you supposed to deliver them?"

"To Stormwell, a port in Canada. But first we were to meet a van outside of Wilmington."

The Hardys looked knowingly at one another. Frank asked what took place at the rendezvous.

"When the van arrived, some guy told us to take a walk and return in an hour," said Miker. "We started out, then doubled back to see what was going on. We spotted those guys loading all sorts of junk into the logs. I was ready to call the deal off right then and there."

"Why didn't you?" Mr. Hardy inquired. "Since it looked crooked, you should have called the police."

"I talked him out of it," Parkins admitted. "I know hoods when I see them. Those guys would never let us quit!"

"And that's all we know," Miker insisted.

"Can you give us a description of any of the men you saw?"

"No," Parkins replied. "It was too dark."

The prisoners were led out of the room. Then the Hardys discussed the situation.

"I'll call the police in Wilmington," Mr. Hardy said. "I would like to find out how the logs got to the dock." He put through a call and the police chief of Wilmington promised to track it down.

"The logs were to be taken to Stormwell," Frank said. "That means one of the *Parrot* ships must be heading there for the pickup."

"You can bet on it," agreed his father. "And our first concern is to prevent information about this from leaking out. We don't want to alert the thieves before the ship docks."

The desk sergeant called out to the Hardys as they hurried from the interrogation room. "It looks as if you fellows are going to get your names in the newspaper today," he announced with a grin.

"What do you mean?" Frank asked.

"Ed Watts, the police reporter for the *Newland Record,* was here about half an hour ago," the sergeant replied. "He checked the police blotter as he usually does. Sure got excited when he learned that you had found the museum loot inside those logs. Didn't even wait for an interview. You should have seen him dash off to make the morning edition with his scoop."

Mr. Hardy rushed to telephone the managing editor of the newspaper. He pleaded with the man not to print the story.

"Sorry," the editor informed him, "but the presses are already rolling. Anyway, it wouldn't do any good. The wire services have picked it up."

The boys were crestfallen when their father told them the situation. He suggested they all return to Bayport and plan a new course of action.

The drivers were released in bail and drove away with their truck, but the logs were kept as evidence.

It was evening by the time the Hardys arrived home. Too exhausted to think clearly, they decided to retire immediately after supper, since Chet had agreed to stay on radio watch one more night.

Before they undressed, a telephone call from the Wilmington police advised that there had been no record of the log shipment. "It obviously was strictly illegal," the officer reported.

Next day the boys rose early and enjoyed a leisurely breakfast, then joined their father who was already at work in his study.

"The morning edition of the *Bayport News* came a little while ago," he said with a frown. "Take a look at the front page, third column."

Frank and Joe looked glum when they saw the headline:

HARDYS FIND MUSEUM LOOT IN HOLLOW LOGS

It read in part: "The Hardys did it again! Officials of the State Museum in Delaware were astounded to learn that the famous Bayport detectives had uncovered an invaluable collection recently stolen from the institution. The loot was cleverly hidden in hollow logs which were being hauled aboard a flatbed truck with Canadian license plates. Police are looking for a possible Canadian contact. . . ."

"This ruins everything!" Joe declared angrily.

Mr. Hardy picked up the phone and placed a call to the Port Authority in Stormwell. He requested any recent information they might have concerning the *Parrot* ships. From the expression on their father's face, the boys concluded that the news was not encouraging.

"You're in for another letdown." Mr. Hardy sighed as he hung up the phone. "The *Black Parrot* was due to dock last night. So far there's no sign of her."

"Someone must have radioed the captain," Frank said, "and told him about our finding the loot."

"He must be making a run for it," Joe added. "And you can be sure Stormwell has seen the last of the *Parrots*."

"If only we had more leads," Mr. Hardy said. "The Stormwell authorities tried to find the location of the ship but to no avail. And where to look next is a problem, because the *Black Parrot* did not report its last position."

"Too bad Parkins and Miker couldn't give us more information about the gang," Joe muttered. He glanced at his brother. "I wonder where the thieves are now."

"Scattered like geese in a hurricane, if they read the newspapers," Frank said glumly.

"As I see it," Mr. Hardy announced, "our only hope of ending this case quickly depends upon one thing."

"What's that, Dad?" Frank asked.

"That your friend Ellis contacts us."

CHAPTER XVII

An Unexpected Visitor

"By this time," Joe said dejectedly, "Ellis might not even be aboard the *Yellow Parrot* any more."

"Possibly," Frank agreed. "He might have decided to escape from the ship. Or the captain could have found out that he had helped us and took him prisoner. But we're just guessing. We have nothing to lose by sticking close to the radio."

That afternoon Chet's jalopy screeched to a halt in front of the Hardy house. The stout youth leaped from his car and jabbed at the doorbell excitedly.

"What's going on?" Joe asked as he admitted his friend to the house. "You look as if you've just discovered the secret of perpetual motion."

"Everybody brace themselves for the unexpected!" Chet declared. "I'll be acclaimed by archaeologists in every corner of the globe!"

"You haven't been digging again?" Joe questioned apprehensively.

"Well—er—yes," his pal admitted with a certain aloofness. "But I made sure there weren't any water mains around."

The commotion brought Mr. Hardy and Frank to the scene. It was then that Chet pulled a small, weathered bowl from his pocket and displayed it proudly.

"Consider yourselves privileged to be among the first to set eyes upon this ancient artifact," he announced. "Study its lines closely."

"Where did you find it?" Frank asked, trying to suppress a grin.

"On the farm," Chet replied.

"How old do you think it is?" Mr. Hardy queried.

"Probably dates back to the preglacial period," Chet replied with a confident air. "A Carbon 14 test will determine its age more exactly."

Aunt Gertrude appeared and stared at Chet's discovery curiously. "Oh, I see you've found it," she said finally.

"Found what?"

"My little sugar bowl," Miss Hardy answered. "Don't you remember? The boys borrowed it when they had a family picnic at your parents' farm."

"I remember now," Joe said. "That must've

been two or three years ago. You were awfully upset when we told you it had been lost."

"Impossible!" Chet shouted indignantly.

Aunt Gertrude hurried away, then reappeared with a bowl in her hand a moment later. It was almost identical in size and shape to Chet's. "You see, it was part of a set. Mercy! Imagine finding the bowl after all this time. But, of course, it's too weathered and cracked to be of use to me now."

Chet's face turned a ruby red. "I—I don't feel too well," he stammered.

The Hardys howled with laughter. Chet dashed out of the house and sped off in his jalopy before the boys could stop him.

"Poor Chet," Joe said with regret. "He took it pretty hard."

"We'll call him up later and apologize," Frank suggested.

After supper the doorbell rang. Mrs. Hardy went to answer it and came back seconds later.

"Fenton, there's a man to see you," she said. "Gertrude doesn't like his looks and is watching him from behind a drape."

Mr. Hardy and the boys accompanied her to the door. Standing on the porch was a man of medium height and weight. He had removed his hat and was clutching it nervously.

"Mr. Hardy?" he quavered.

"That's right."

"You gotta help me. I'm in serious trouble."

The Hardys led the caller to the study and offered him a chair.

"Now suppose you tell me what kind of trouble you're in," asked Mr. Hardy, "and how I can help you."

"My name is Barney Egart," the man started. He seemed reluctant to go on for a moment, but then continued. "I got myself into a terrible mess."

"What mess?" Frank questioned.

"Going with those guys to the State Museum," Egart replied. "You've got to believe me! It was my first job with the gang!"

His statement struck the Hardys like a thunderbolt.

"You mean you were in on the robbery?" Joe exclaimed.

"Where's the rest of the gang?" Frank wanted to know.

"On their way to Canada. After the stuff was loaded inside the logs, we split up. Orders were to meet in Stormwell for the payoff."

"Go on," Mr. Hardy said quietly.

Egart shifted in his chair nervously. "When I saw all the news about the robbery, I chickened out of the Stormwell meeting. So I decided to come here."

"Why?" Mr. Hardy inquired.

"I don't have any friends who can help me. No money. Nothing!" came the reply. "Your reputation is well known. You see that a guy gets a break. So when I read you were connected with the investigation, I decided to talk to you."

"How did you get involved with the gang in the first place?" Joe asked.

"I was in Wilmington a few days ago looking for work," Egart explained. "Things were pretty bleak. Then I ran into a guy I'd met in California once. Name is Starker."

Frank turned to his father. "That's the big fellow who was employed at the museum in Philadelphia as a gardener!"

"I don't know anything about that," Egart commented. "All I know is that the guy asked me if I wanted to make some easy money. Said his friends needed an extra man for a job coming up. I was too broke to turn it down."

At Mr. Hardy's request, Egart gave him a description of six other men who made up the gang. He said that since it was his first meeting with them, he knew nothing about their operations, or if they had a permanent hideout.

"Do you know anything about two ships named the *Yellow Parrot* and the *Black Parrot?*" Frank queried.

The man appeared surprised by the question. "I overheard a couple of the guys talking about them," he said. "They pick up the loot and make the payoffs. And I can tell you this. From what I've heard, the gang doesn't know any more about

They gazed at the message excitedly

the ships than I do. They're hired to steal the stuff and deliver it, that's all."

"It's a safe setup," Frank said. "Whoever wants the DeGraw collection doesn't risk getting caught at the scene."

When the questioning was over, Mr. Hardy said, "I promise to do whatever I can for you. But the first thing is to turn yourself in."

"You—you mean to the police?" Egart stammered.

"Yes. Otherwise there's nothing I can do to help. Also, the fact that you surrendered on your own will be to your advantage."

Reluctantly Egart agreed. The Hardys drove him to Bayport Police Headquarters, where he officially gave himself up. Chief Collig was off duty, but quickly appeared in response to a telephone call.

"I'll get this out on the teletype right away," the chief said when Mr. Hardy gave him Egart's descriptions of the men.

When they returned home Frank elected to stand by the radio. He carefully tuned the receiver to the prearranged frequency, then settled back in his chair with a book.

It was almost midnight when a faint signal in Morse code crackled from the receiver. Frank sat bolt upright in his chair and copied down the dots and dashes. Deciphered, the message read: *Ellis 0200 GMT tomorrow.*

Frank rushed to awaken his father and Joe. They gazed at the message excitedly.

"It must mean that Ellis is going to contact us at oh-two-hundred hours Greenwich Meridian Time tomorrow," Joe concluded. "That would be nine o'clock our time."

The following day dragged on slowly for the boys. Then, as the appointed hour arrived, the Hardys crowded around the radio receiver. Soon they began to hear: *dit dit-dah-dit-dit dit-dah-dit-dit dit-dit* . . .

Frank jotted down the message: *Ellis need help. Urgent. Will transmit 200 KC 1700 CW to 2100 GMT daily. Should pick up at Cambrian. Must go.*

"He's in trouble!" Joe exclaimed.

CHAPTER XVIII

A Hidden Target

FRANK transmitted an immediate reply, but there was no response from Ellis.

"Maybe our equipment isn't powerful enough to reach his receiver," Joe said. "We don't know how far away he is."

Mr. Hardy studied the message. "Ellis will be transmitting on a frequency of two hundred kilocycles," he observed. "But for what reason? And I've forgotten what the CW means."

"*Continuous* or *Carrier Wave*," Frank explained. "It's the modulation of these waves that make it possible to transmit."

"Quite right."

"What it amounts to, Dad," Joe put in, "is that Ellis will be transmitting a continuous signal on which we can take a directional bearing or home in with an aircraft radio compass."

"And 'Should pick up at Cambrian,'" Mr. Hardy concluded, "must mean that you can begin receiving the signal in the vicinity of that island."

"Exactly," agreed Frank.

"Then there's no time to lose," his father decided. "We must go there as soon as possible."

"Shall we use your plane?" Joe asked.

"I've another idea," Frank said. "Dan Tiller's amphibian is better suited for an over-the-water search. We can offer to hire his services when we get to Cambrian. If he's not available, there'll be other amphibians for charter."

"Good," Mr. Hardy said. "Right now, I'd better telephone the airline and make reservations. By the way, ask Chet if he wants to come along. We're going to need all the help we can get. I'll get a seat for him too."

"Great!" Frank said. "I'll call him as soon as you're finished."

Chet was still a bit miffed at the way they had laughed about the sugar bowl. But his attitude quickly changed when he heard of the proposed trip to Cambrian Island.

"When do we leave?" he shouted excitedly.

"We'll let you know just as soon as Dad has our reservations confirmed. It'll be tomorrow morning some time."

Soon the phone rang and the boys hurried to Mr. Hardy's study. He was just putting down the phone. "Everything's set," he said. "We'll depart tomorrow at eight A.M. from La Guardia. Jack can fly us there."

The atmosphere at breakfast the next morning was charged with suspense. Although Mrs. Hardy did not share her family's excitement regarding the trip, she gallantly took it in stride.

Aunt Gertrude, however, could not restrain herself. "Mark my words!" she exclaimed brusquely. "Don't press your luck too far. Nothing good can come of this foolish trip!"

"Where's your spirit, Aunty?" Frank teased.

"Humph!" was her only answer.

After urging the two women not to worry, Fenton Hardy and his sons drove off to pick up Chet at the Morton farm, then hastened to Bayport Airport. Jack Wayne was already waiting, and soon they were in the air, heading for New York.

"There will be a slight delay because of heavy air traffic," Jack announced as they neared their destination.

Upon landing, the Hardys and Chet hurried to the terminal building. Their flight to Miami was being announced over the public-address system. They checked in their luggage and boarded the jet.

"I didn't think we'd be seeing Cambrian again so soon," Joe remarked as the aircraft lifted off the ground.

"Let's hope we'll find Tiller there," Frank added.

In Miami, the four changed planes as scheduled and departed on the last leg of their journey.

It was midafternoon when the plane touched down on the runway at Cambrian. By telephone Mr. Hardy made arrangements for them to stay at a new hotel located near the airport.

"Dad," Frank said, "Joe and I would like to go to the other side of the field to see if we can locate Tiller. We'll meet you at the hotel later."

"Certainly. Go ahead. Chet can stay with me and help with the luggage."

The boys dashed out of the terminal building and headed toward the south side of the field. It was in that area that Tiller had parked his amphibian after they had returned from Tambio.

"There he is!" Joe yelled, pointing.

"Boy, am I glad we found him," Frank said and called hello to the pilot.

Tiller was surprised to see the Hardys.

"What are you fellows doing here?" he asked with a wide grin. "I thought you were back in Bayport hunting criminals!"

"We were," Joe replied.

"Have any trouble repairing the engine?" Frank inquired.

"None at all," the pilot assured him. "Spare crankcases are one thing I'm not short of. It was just a matter of replacing it."

"That's great," Joe put in, "because we'd like to hire your services."

"I'm available. What is it you want me to do?"

The boys told him about Ellis's message and of the possibility of using his signal to locate the *Yellow Parrot.*

"And you say he'll be transmitting on CW between the hours of 1700 and 2100 Greenwich Time?" Tiller queried.

"Right," Frank answered. "What's the time zone difference here?"

"Cambrian is three hours earlier than Greenwich," Tiller replied. "So that would make it two P.M. to six P.M. local time." He glanced at his watch. "If your friend is keeping to his schedule, he should still be transmitting. Want to take a trial hop in my plane and see if we can pick up the signal?"

"Sure. That's a good idea," Frank said.

"I'll go and give Dad a ring at the hotel," Joe volunteered. "Be right back."

Ten minutes later they were streaking down the runway on take-off in the amphibian.

Tiller climbed to five thousand feet, leveled off, then tuned his radio compass receiver to two hundred kilocycles. There was no response.

"If the ship's a great distance away," Frank remarked, "the signal will be very weak."

Tiller increased power and eased the nose of the plane upwards. "I'll climb to a higher altitude," he said.

The amphibian was approaching ten thousand feet when the indicator needle on the radio compass began to flicker. A low, steady humming sound came from the speaker of the receiver.

"We're getting something!" Joe exclaimed.

"It *must* be the signal from the *Yellow Parrot*," Frank said.

The pilot watched the instrument. "The needle is reacting sluggishly," he observed. "The ship's quite a distance away. But we can determine the direction."

"Have any idea about how far?" asked Joe.

"No. But I'll fly a *time-distance* problem. It will only give us a rough estimate. However, that's better than nothing."

As Tiller began the maneuver, he explained that the procedure involved flying in a direction which would be exactly at *right angles* to that of the ship. "The heading is then maintained until the radio compass shows at least a 10-degree change in relative bearing," he said.

The boys listened eagerly as Tiller went on, "This change in bearing, together with the time flown in order to obtain it, is used in a very simple mathematical formula to get the distance to the source of the signal, or in this case, the *Yellow Parrot*."

Several minutes passed. Then the pilot jotted down some figures.

"According to my calculation," he announced finally, "the ship is from three hundred and fifty to four hundred miles away."

Joe let out a low whistle. "Does your plane have enough fuel to make it there and back?" he queried.

"Barely," Tiller replied. "But I have a long-range tank I can install in the cabin. It'll give us plenty of reserve."

"There's one snag," Joe interjected. "Won't the tank cut down the number of passengers you can carry?"

"Yes," the pilot agreed. "I'll be limited to two."

"Dad and Chet won't be happy to hear that," Frank muttered.

Tiller returned to the airport. After parking his airplane, he asked, "When do you want to make this flight?"

"Tomorrow, if possible," Frank said. "But I want to be sure you realize the danger. The crewmen aboard the *Yellow Parrot* are rough customers. If we should run into trouble and get caught—"

"Don't worry about me," Tiller interrupted.

The boys rejoined their father and Chet at the hotel and told them about their flight.

"And you say the long-range tank will permit only two passengers," Mr. Hardy said. "I've a feeling you'll suggest that Chet and I go and you two stay behind." He winked at Frank.

Chet let out a whoop and patted Mr. Hardy on the back.

"Well, not exactly," Joe said.

"We know the *Yellow Parrot*," Frank explained. "It's better that we go."

Chet sat down, looking disappointed.

"If you locate the ship, you must promise to be careful," Mr. Hardy told his sons. "Don't try boarding the freighter. Get what information Ellis has and return here as soon as possible."

"We will," Joe promised.

It was late the following morning when Tiller telephoned the boys to tell them that he had just finished installing the long-range tank.

"That's great," Frank said. "Let's plan to take off a few minutes before Ellis is scheduled to begin sending his signal."

"Okay."

Mr. Hardy and Chet accompanied Frank and Joe to the airport. As departure time neared, Tiller started the engines and his two passengers climbed aboard the plane.

"Good luck!" Mr. Hardy shouted above the noise of the propellers. "And remember what I told you!"

His sons waved from a side window as Tiller taxied toward the active runway.

Soon the amphibian was climbing out to sea. Then it turned on a southerly heading.

"It's exactly two o'clock," Joe announced, glancing at his watch. "Ellis should be transmitting."

The pilot switched on his radio compass receiver and tuned to the proper frequency. A low, humming sound crackled from the speaker. Gradually the needle of the instrument started to seek out the source of the signal.

"A course of 165 degrees should take us in the right direction for the moment," Tiller said. "The indication will become more accurate as we get closer to the ship."

Three hours went by. The boys watched the radio compass as it grew more and more sensitive to Ellis's signal.

"I'm going to work another *time-distance* problem," the pilot declared.

He swung the plane onto a new heading, and within a few minutes, completed his calculation. "We've got about eighty miles to go," he concluded.

The boys tingled with excitement. Less than half an hour had gone by when Frank pointed directly ahead.

"Cumulus clouds!" he exclaimed. "That could mean an island or a group of islands."

"Right," Tiller agreed. "And according to our radio compass, we're headed toward them."

As they continued, small rocky islets began to slide beneath them. Ahead, a mass of somewhat larger islands came into view.

"We're getting a strong signal," the pilot said. "We must be very near the ship."

"Stay on your present course and keep going,"

Frank said. "If the crew spots our plane, we don't want them to know we're searching for the *Yellow Parrot*."

An instant later the needle of the radio compass whirled around and pointed toward the tail of the aircraft.

"We've just passed over the ship!" Tiller shouted.

The boys quickly scanned the islands below. They saw no sign of the freighter, but noticed an odd-shaped island with a narrow inlet that was heavily covered with vegetation.

"I've a hunch the *Yellow Parrot* is hidden down there," Joe said.

"So do I," Frank agreed. "Let's land and take a look."

Tiller continued on his original course for a few more minutes, then descended to within a few feet of the water and turned back toward the islands.

"We'll stay down low to avoid being spotted," he told them. "Then I'll land about a mile out and taxi the rest of the way."

"Okay," Frank said. "The island we want is in the center of the group. After dark, Joe and I will use your rubber raft and paddle to the inlet we saw."

After a smooth water landing, Tiller and the boys settled down to await sunset.

Tiller reached behind his seat. "Here's some

chow I brought," he said. "And over there are cans of soda."

"Am I glad you thought of food," Joe replied with a chuckle. "This flight sure stimulated my appetite!"

After they had eaten, they talked until it was dark. Then the pilot inflated the raft and eased it over the side.

"Lots of luck," he said in a hushed voice as Frank and Joe started toward their objective.

The next hour was spent weaving in and out of a series of small islands. Finally the Hardys had the inlet in sight. They could make out the vague image of a ship anchored beneath a camouflage net covered with vegetation.

"It's the *Yellow Parrot!*" Joe said excitedly.

"Let's paddle closer," Frank whispered. "But we'd better stay near the shore for cover."

They came within a hundred yards of the ship and Frank's right hand, gripping the paddle, dipped deep into the water. Their eyes were strained at the figures moving about the deck.

"We can't make a sound," Frank whispered. "Feather your paddle in the water, Joe, don't lift it out!"

"Roger. I see they have guards posted near the rail."

Just then a sharp whack hit the side of the raft. There was a swishing sound in the water, and something grabbed Frank's paddle just below his fingers.

"A shark!" he cried out. He had hardly uttered the warning when a huge dorsal fin knifed under the bottom of the raft, half-lifting it out of the water. The boys tried to hang on, but were hurled over the lip and into the briny sea.

Silence was now out of the question. Frank and Joe knew that they must kick, scream, and flail their arms in an effort to scare the shark away.

"Swim for it!" Joe shrieked.

The shark made another pass, brushing past him with a tail slap which made Joe feel as if the end of the world had come.

The Hardys were too terror-stricken to notice what was going on at the ship's deck. The noise had alerted the crew. Bright beams of light pierced the darkness and swept toward the raft.

"Do you hear something?" yelled a crewman aboard the freighter.

"Someone's out there!" shouted another. "And a shark's after him!"

"Get a rifle!" came a third voice.

As Frank and Joe struggled frantically to reach the shore, a shot whizzed past Frank and hit the shark with a thud.

Joe, who was behind his brother, saw the monster roll belly up and stain the sea with red, in the glare of the spotlight.

An instant later the boys reached a patch of sandy beach. They scrambled ashore and glanced around for a place to hide.

"Head for cover!" Frank whispered, pointing to a clump of rocks nearby.

Before they could make a run for it, a group of bronze-skinned natives seemed to appear from nowhere. They quickly surrounded the youths. There was no escape!

CHAPTER XIX

The Pirate King

THE Hardys were seized and marched off. The group walked along the beach for a short distance, then turned onto a trail leading inland.

"Where are you taking us?" Joe demanded.

The natives did not speak. Instead, they gestured to the boys to keep moving.

After traveling about a mile, they came to a village tucked in a valley ahead. The community was comprised of small stone buildings, boxlike in shape. Coconut palms dotted the area.

In the center of the village was a medieval-looking structure. The boys were led toward it.

"Look!" Joe exclaimed in disbelief.

Two guards flanked a set of heavy wooden, arch-shaped doors with massive iron hinges. They wore conquistador-type helmets and breastplates, which bore the bright-red symbol of the twisted claw!

At a signal from one of the natives, the guards

pushed open the doors and ordered the prisoners inside.

The interior of the building was magnificent. The walls soared upwards and met in a series of gentle arches. These, combined with towering columns and polished stone floors, gave the area a palatial appearance.

"Amazing!" Joe whispered.

"I could do without it!" Frank muttered.

They were marched toward another set of wooden doors flanked by helmeted guards. On the wall above were carved the letters ETC.

"Empire of the Twisted Claw!" Frank muttered, recalling the rare volume they had seen in the New York bookstore.

The doors were pushed open to reveal a large room which looked much like a medieval banquet hall. Seated on the far side on a throne was a man wearing a fur-collared red robe. His aquiline nose jutted out from between a set of dark, glacial eyes. Standing to his right was Rawlin, first mate of the *Yellow Parrot!*

The man rose and stared at the boys menacingly. "What have we here?" he shouted. "Prisoners?"

Rawlin gazed at Frank and Joe as if he were seeing ghosts. "I know those kids!" he yelled. "They're the Hardy boys!"

"Sons of Fenton Hardy the detective?" asked the man in the robe.

"Yeah!" Rawlin answered. "They sailed aboard our ship once. I didn't know who they were at the time. Then we got the message from the *Black Parrot* saying that the loot from the State Museum heist had been found by the Hardys."

"Tell me more!" the man in the robe said in an ice-cold voice.

"Well, I put two and two together. I asked for their descriptions and, sure enough, it checked with the kids who jumped ship at Tambio."

"News travels fast, doesn't it!" snapped Joe.

The red-robed man seated himself again in chilly composure. "I am Cartoll, king of this island," he announced. "I demand to know how you got here!"

"You don't really expect us to tell you!" Frank shot back.

"We were sightseeing," Joe wisecracked. "It's a nice island."

Rawlin fumed. "Let me take care of these guys!"

"Calm yourself," Cartoll ordered with a smirk. "I admire audacity. However, I've no time to question them now." He clapped his hands.

Two guards responded. "Take the prisoners to the east tower room!" Cartoll commanded.

"I still think we oughta find out how they got here first!" Rawlin protested. "There might be others!"

"It's obvious they came by boat or plane," Cartoll concluded. "Have your men conduct a search of the area as soon as it is light."

"If only there was some way to warn Tiller," Frank thought frantically as he and his brother were led away by the guards.

The east tower room was situated at the top of a long, winding stone stairway. One of the guards unlocked the door and ordered the boys inside. The other one brought some bread and a jug of water, then the door was shut behind them.

When their eyes grew accustomed to the gloom, they were startled to see an elderly man with shaggy gray hair and a beard seated at a wooden table.

"Are you prisoners of Cartoll too?" he asked in a weak voice. "I have not seen you before."

"Yes," Frank replied glumly. "And who are you?"

"Leroy Ellis."

Frank and Joe looked at each other in surprise, then Frank introduced himself and his brother. "Any relation to Clay Ellis?" he added.

"He's my son. You know him?"

"We've met him not long ago. Why are you a prisoner?"

"Because I refuse to help Cartoll with his crazy schemes. And I'm being used as a hostage so my son won't go to the authorities."

"So that's why Clay wouldn't tell us anything," Joe said, munching on a piece of bread.

"Perhaps you can tell us what's going on around here," Frank said. "Who *is* this Cartoll?"

The old man explained that Cartoll was the great-great-great grandson of a notorious eighteenth-century pirate who had established a kingdom on the island.

"We read about him and his Empire of the Twisted Claw in an old book," Joe interrupted.

"If you're familiar with that part of the story," Ellis said, "I'll bring you up to date."

He explained that he came upon the island more than a year before while sailing his ketch around the Caribbean. He was accompanied by his son, who was on vacation from his job as radioman for a reputable shipping firm. They were impressed with the old buildings of the village and the friendliness of the natives.

During their stay, Cartoll arrived on the island and declared himself heir to his ancestor's kingdom. He forced the natives to be his subjects and revived the Empire of the Twisted Claw.

"He's mad and must be stopped!" Ellis insisted.

"What about the *Parrot* ships?" asked Frank.

The old man scowled. "Cartoll owns the ships and uses them for smuggling purposes. It's that scoundrel's way of financing his so-called royal enterprises."

Frank went on, "Do you know why he's so determined to get his hands on the DeGraw collection?"

"It's another of his crazy quirks," Ellis replied. "The items in that collection were owned by the original pirate king. They were being brought here to the island by a galleon when a sudden storm came up and sank the ship."

"And now Cartoll thinks the stuff belongs to him by reason of inheritance?" Joe queried.

The old man nodded. "Of course the idea is absurd. But such things are meaningless to a person of his mentality."

After their talk, the Hardys' thoughts turned to the possibility of escape.

"Your chances are slim," Ellis warned. "There are too many guards inside the palace."

Joe pointed to the only window in the room. It was a small, lancet-shaped opening covered with metal bars. "Maybe we can get out through there," he suggested.

Ellis smiled. "I had the same idea once." He reached inside his sleeve and pulled out a pointed piece of metal about the size of a pencil. "I began using this to dig away the stone around two of the bars. After that, I could stick my head through and realized escape was hopeless. There's a forty-foot drop to the ground."

The boys examined the window and saw where Ellis had scraped away the stone at the base of the bars. He had cleverly filled the depressions with loose dirt to prevent his work from being discovered.

Joe pushed away the bars and gazed down. "It is quite a drop," he said.

"I have an idea," Frank put in. "We'll tie our jackets and belts together to form a line. It won't reach all the way to the ground, but at least it'll lessen the height."

"I have a blanket you can use," Ellis added.

The boys quickly knotted the articles together. Then Frank estimated its length. This will take us within fifteen feet of the ground."

"A cinch," Joe commented with a grin.

Frank glanced at his watch. "It'll be daylight within a couple of hours. We'll have to work fast."

Frantically the Hardys dug away the stone until the lower ends of two more bars were exposed. Then they pushed and pulled with all their strength until the upper ends loosened and tore free.

"All set?" Joe asked as he secured the line to one of the remaining bars.

"I—I'd like to go with you," Ellis said shakily. "But I don't know if I can make it."

"We're not leaving you behind," Frank said firmly. "You can do it. My brother and I will go first. We'll be waiting to help break your fall."

The Hardys slid down their makeshift line, then dropped the remaining distance to the ground.

Next, Mr. Ellis emerged from the window above. He gripped the line and started to descend.

But at the halfway point he came to a halt. The man obviously was frightened.

"Don't stop now," Frank muttered anxiously.

There was a short pause. Then Ellis continued and finally made a soft landing with the boys' help.

"Now what?" Joe asked in a hushed voice.

"Let's head back to where the *Yellow Parrot* is anchored," Frank urged. "Somehow we've got to get hold of a raft or a boat and warn Dan Tiller."

Dawn was breaking as the trio dashed out of the village and along the rugged trail leading to the beach.

Upon reaching their destination, they were stunned by what they saw. Tied to a mooring close to the *Yellow Parrot* was Tiller's amphibian!

"Dan's been captured!" Joe exclaimed.

Frank was too shocked to speak. He stared at the plane, realizing that their only means of escape had fallen into the hands of Cartoll!

CHAPTER XX

Island Rescue

At the sound of men approaching from behind, the boys and Mr. Ellis quickly hid in some brush.

"I don't like what you're planning to do," came Rawlin's voice. "It's too risky."

"Your opinion couldn't interest me less," a second man replied.

"That's Cartoll!" Joe whispered.

"But you already have most of the DeGraw collection," Rawlin went on. "And the gang you hired has been arrested. Why take chances?"

"You don't understand," Cartoll countered. "That portion of the collection at the Norwood Museum in Connecticut is of special interest to me. The armor was made for my ancestor's exclusive use. I must have it."

"So you're bent on stealing the stuff yourself," Rawlin said in disgust.

"Not exactly. You and some of the crew are

going to help me. And thanks to the Hardys, we have a plane at our disposal. We'll be there in no time!"

The men walked by the hidden trio. They halted when they reached the beach. The Hardys could still overhear their conversation.

"But I've never done anything like that before," Rawlin protested.

"There's always a first time," Cartoll said sarcastically. "Don't worry," he added. "With the gang captured, the museum will surely be off its guard. We won't have any trouble."

Rawlin shouted to a crewman on the deck of the *Yellow Parrot* and ordered him to bring a dinghy ashore. Soon the men were being rowed out to the ship.

Frank's and Joe's pulses quickened as they waited and watched. Suddenly Tiller appeared on the deck. He was being pushed along by two hefty crewmen. They ordered him over the side and into another dinghy. Then they took him to his amphibian.

"Tiller's removing the long-range tank," Joe observed after a while.

"Right. He's making room for Cartoll and his cohorts," Frank added. "But he still has enough reserve in his main tanks to reach Cambrian and refuel before going on."

"Maybe he'll try to make a break for it there," Joe said.

"I doubt that your friend will get a chance to escape," Mr. Ellis warned. "Cartoll is clever. He'll be watching like a hawk!"

More than two hours had passed when the Hardys saw Cartoll, Rawlin, and three other men leave the ship and board the plane. Then Tiller started the engines and taxied out to clear water. He applied take-off power and the craft left a churning wake behind as it sped along. Soon it rose off the water and disappeared to the north.

Frank sighed. "We're in bad shape! Tiller and his plane might never come back here, and even if Cartoll brought him back, how could we contact him?"

"Might as well resign ourselves to being hermits from now on," Joe quipped in dark humor.

Mr. Ellis turned to the boys. "I've got an idea," he said slowly. "There's a good chance it might work."

"What's that?" Frank inquired.

"I have earned the respect of many of the natives, including the village leader. Their fear of Cartoll prevented them from getting together and ousting the tyrant. Now that he's away, maybe I can talk them into action!"

"If only you could!" Joe said excitedly.

"It's awfully chancy," Frank warned.

"But it's our only alternative. I'm going back to the village," Ellis declared. "At least it's worth a try."

"We'll go with you," Frank said.

"No, it's better I go alone," the man insisted. "You fellows keep an eye on the *Yellow Parrot*. Maybe you'll spot my son." He scrambled to his feet and disappeared down the trail.

The Hardys grew more impatient as the hours dragged by. All was quiet aboard the ship. Sunset was less than an hour away when the boys heard sounds of commotion from the direction of the village. They sprang to their feet just as two guards in shiny breastplates came running down the trail. The young detectives flung themselves at the men and caught them above the knees. Their opponents somersaulted into the air and crashed to the ground.

A split second later two more guards appeared. The boys attacked. Locked in a struggle, they and the men tumbled down the trail and onto the sandy beach. A crowd of natives arrived and seized the guards.

"It worked!" Mr. Ellis shouted joyfully as he pushed his way through the group. "We've got the scoundrels on the run!"

"Look!" Joe yelled to his brother as he pointed toward the *Yellow Parrot*.

Frank turned to see the ship getting underway.

"My son is still aboard!" the old man cried out.

A minute later an amphibian, much larger than Tiller's, roared low overhead. It turned and landed on the water nearby.

As the plane taxied toward the beach, its aft cabin door sprang open. The boys were startled to see their father's head appear. "Hello, sons!" he shouted. "Are you all right?"

"Starved, but okay otherwise," Frank called back.

A rubber raft tossed over the side. Mr. Hardy climbed into it. Then Chet emerged and joined him. Together they paddled ashore.

"Are we glad to see you!" Joe declared with relief. "But how did you know we were in trouble?"

"I have an excellent view of the airport from my hotel room in Cambrian," the detective explained, "and happened to spot Tiller's amphibian come in for a landing. Naturally, I thought you had returned. When Chet and I went to the field, we were startled to see the plane taking off again. I knew something was wrong."

The detective said that he then contacted air-sea rescue and an aircraft was made available for an immediate search.

"Luckily," Mr. Hardy added, "Ellis hadn't stopped sending his signal."

"Looks as if you've had a bit of excitement around here," Chet observed. He stared at the captured guards. "Who are these characters in the tin coats?"

Frank and Joe told him about their recent adventure. Then they introduced Mr. Ellis.

"We owe a lot to you and your son," Mr. Hardy told the gray-haired man.

"Thank you," Mr. Ellis replied. "But Clay is still aboard the ship. What can we do?"

"Don't worry," Mr. Hardy said. "I'm going to request an international alert. The *Parrots* will be seized wherever they try to put into port. Your son will be all right."

Darkness was approaching rapidly. Frank glanced at his watch. "We still have Cartoll to deal with," he interjected. "He and his men have several hours head start on us. We'll have to move fast!"

Mr. Ellis joined the Hardys on the flight back to Cambrian. While en route, the pilot contacted Miami on his high-frequency transmitter at Mr. Hardy's request. He asked that a message, warning about the intended robbery, be relayed to the authorities in Norwood. A full description of the thieves was included.

Upon arriving at their destination, Mr. Hardy and his party quickly gathered their luggage. After saying good-by to Mr. Ellis, they boarded the last shuttle flight of the evening to Miami.

"I've never traveled so many miles in so short a time before," Chet remarked wearily as the plane approached the Florida city.

In Miami, Mr. Hardy telephoned Jack Wayne and instructed him to meet them at La Guardia.

Then he and the boys boarded a jetliner and were soon speeding northward.

The flight to New York was smooth and fast. Jack was waiting when they arrived and flew them directly to Norwood. There a patrol car was standing by to take Mr. Hardy and the boys to the museum.

"We caught all but one of the thieves," the policeman announced as they drove, "thanks to the information you sent us."

"Which one of them got away?" Frank asked quickly.

"I don't know. You'll have to ask the chief," the officer replied. "They were real amateurs. Broke open a door at the rear of the museum and set off an alarm hooked up to headquarters."

"The gang forced a pilot by the name of Tiller to fly them here," Joe said anxiously. "Any news from him?"

"He landed his plane on the lake near here. Later a state trooper happened to spot it anchored close to shore. He investigated and found the pilot tied and gagged in the cabin. The fellow's okay and is at headquarters."

When they arrived at the museum, several patrol cars and a police van were parked at the curb. Inside the van were Rawlin and the three crewmen. Cartoll was missing!

"Where's your boss?" Joe demanded.

"I don't know," Rawlin snarled. "And don't ask me any more questions because I'm not talking."

Frank rubbed his chin dubiously. "Cartoll couldn't have vanished into thin air!" He turned to the police chief. "Mind if we go inside the building and have a look around?"

"Go ahead," the officer answered. "But I doubt that you'll find anything."

Joe and Frank entered the museum and hurried to the exhibit room where the DeGraw collection was displayed.

The room was dark. Frank found the switch and turned on the lights. The boys looked around. Everything was intact. On the far side of the room, armor engraved with the symbol of the twisted claw stood on a pedestal.

As they turned to leave, Joe suddenly grabbed his brother's arm. "Hold on!" he whispered. "I might be seeing things, but I'm sure that figure on the pedestal moved!"

Cautiously they walked toward the spot. Frank stepped forward and lifted the visor.

A face stared at him. *Cartoll!* With a curse, the man sprang at the youths. A violent struggle followed. Joe screamed for help. The noise brought Mr. Hardy and several policemen to the scene.

"What's going on here?" one of the officers demanded.

The boys hauled the metal-clad man to his feet. "Meet Cartoll!" Joe declared.

Frank pulled the helmet from their captive's head. "Clever way to avoid being captured. And he almost got away with it."

Cartoll was furious. "You'll regret having meddled in my affairs!" he shouted. "Too bad Starker didn't succeed in squashing you like an ant in the Philadelphia museum."

"That's another charge against you," Joe said. "Attempted murder."

As the police marched the prisoner away, Mr. Hardy held up a box-shaped object. At one end was what appeared to be a photographic lens.

"What's that?" Frank inquired.

"It's the secret as to how the museum thieves avoided setting off the photoelectric alarm systems during some of their robberies," his father replied. "Rawlin and his cohorts were carrying a supply of these when the police caught them."

"How does the gadget work?" asked Joe.

"You know that the alarm system operates by aiming a beam of light at a photoelectric cell," Mr. Hardy began. "The cell and light source are on opposite sides of the room. As long as the beam is not interrupted by someone walking through it, nothing happens. But if the beam is broken, off goes the alarm."

Joe nodded. "I get it," he said. "That box you're holding is a device which produces a beam of light. If aimed at the photoelectric cell, it simply replaces the original light source across the room."

"Exactly," his father said. "Then the thieves were free to move around the area without setting off the alarm."

"Simple," Frank muttered. "But not all the museums had this type of system!"

"True, but one of the gang's members was an expert in alarm technology. They tackled each one according to how it was set up.

"Once that problem was solved," Mr. Hardy continued, "the rest was comparatively easy. Some of their hirelings got jobs at the museums they planned to rob. They punctured the gas masks, making sure the knockout fumes would be effective."

"Like Starker, who worked as a gardener," Joe interjected.

"Right. In other cases they threatened the guards to let them in. They used a different approach each time, and that's what made the case so hard to crack."

"There's one more thing that bothers me," Frank said. "What caused that shell hole in the *Yellow Parrot?*"

Mr. Hardy grinned. "I found that out, too. She was shot at by a Central American smuggler patrol boat one night, but got away without being identified."

At that moment Chet wandered into the museum. He had been dozing in the squad car and was rubbing his eyes. "Find any clues?" he asked with a yawn.

"A few," Frank quipped. "You're a little bit late."

"Why didn't you wake me up? I was supposed to help you with this case."

Mr. Hardy smiled. "We're all pretty tired. Let's head for home. The mystery is ended."

The boys nodded. Frank and Joe had no idea at that time that a new mystery would soon take up all their time, namely *The Disappearing Floor*.

It was morning when they arrived in Bayport. Mr. Morton greeted them when they dropped off Chet at the farm.

"I'm glad to see my son's back," he said. "I've lots of work for him."

"But I need a chance to recuperate!" Chet protested.

"Okay," his father replied. "I'll give you till tomorrow. Then you'd better start turning over a patch of crabgrass on the front lawn."

"That should be right down your alley, Chet." Joe laughed. "You might be lucky and discover another sugar bowl!"